A WIFE
FOR THE
RANCHER

HIGH COUNTRY RANCH SERIES

A WIFE
FOR THE
RANCHER

JODY HEDLUND

NORTHERN LIGHTS PRESS

A Wife for the Rancher
Northern Lights Press
© 2024 by Jody Hedlund
Jody Hedlund Print Edition
ISBN: 979-8-9896277-2-1

Jody Hedlund www.jodyhedlund.com

Scripture quotations are taken from the King James Version of the Bible.

This is a work of historical reconstruction; the appearances of certain historical figures are accordingly inevitable. All other characters are products of the author's imagination. Any resemblance to actual events or locales or persons, living or dead, is entirely coincidental.

Cover Design by Hannah Linder
Cover images from Shutterstock

1

NEW YORK CITY

AUGUST 1879

Genevieve Hollis read the *New York Herald* personal advertisement: *Colorado rancher with homestead, 25 years old, 6 feet 2 inches tall, 180 pounds, brown hair, brown eyes. Seeking wife to be a mother for newborn infant. Must be loyal, faithful, hardworking, and independent.*

Independent. Oh, to be independent.

Genevieve peeked out of the supply closet, where she was standing with Constance.

Bishop was still in the same spot near the orphanage entrance, where he always took up his post. In a dark suit, the silver-haired man was still occupied with the new Mark Twain novel she'd purchased for him on the drive over to Open Door Asylum, and he hadn't realized yet that she'd disappeared into the closet and was speaking privately with her friend.

Or if he had noticed, hopefully he assumed she was tallying up the clothing donations and making a list of the depleted items.

"I don't know which one to choose." Constance was holding a second advertisement she'd clipped from the newspaper, along with the letters she'd received from both men. "The rancher from Colorado or the stockman from Kansas."

"Either sounds really lovely." Genevieve fingered the advertisement from the Colorado rancher again. "I am sure you will be happy regardless of what you decide." Because Constance was happy all the time no matter her circumstances, and nothing ever seemed to cause her any despondency.

The humidity and heat of the August day were heavy already at the morning hour, leaving a mustiness in the air of the old, terraced home that had been transformed into the orphanage a decade ago. The closet, lined with shelves, was particularly stuffy, but it was the best place for a private conversation that Bishop couldn't hear.

"Which would you choose if you were me?" Constance whispered.

While Genevieve shared the same dark brown, almost-black hair color as Constance, that was where the similarities in their appearances ended. Frazzled wisps of Constance's dark hair curled around her flushed face, but Genevieve didn't have a single hair out of place. Every strand was smoothed back and coiffed as elegantly as always.

Constance was larger boned and wearing a worn skirt and dull blouse, whereas Genevieve was petite and slender, made more so by her corset, which was laced tightly to accommodate the fashionable, slim-fitting princess skirt and cuirass bodice. Constance had warm brown eyes that were always so expressive. Genevieve described her own blue-gray eyes as icy, the color of a winter sky. While Constance's skin was sun-kissed, Genevieve's never felt the warmth of sunshine and was pale and unblemished.

Not only were their appearances different, but their social statuses were completely opposite too. Constance was a poor young woman and one of the house mothers for the Open Door Asylum. After working in the orphanage for the past few years, she was finally ready to have a family of her own.

Genevieve would be sad to lose her unlikely friend and ally, but Constance deserved to have everything she'd dreamed of. Additionally, with the cutting back of the orphanage staff, Constance would be out of a job and a place to live by the end of the month. Rather than trying to find new employment in the city, Constance had opted instead to get married.

The young woman was fetching enough that she surely could have found a husband without resorting to such drastic measures as responding to the matrimonial advertisements in the newspaper. But Constance had been talking for some time about leaving the overcrowded city, especially after hearing so much about the West from the agents who placed orphans there.

Now that she had the opportunity to go, she was taking it.

Genevieve tried to quell the envy that rose too often of late. As one of the wealthiest women in New York City, she knew she shouldn't complain about her life, especially when she considered the twenty or so children currently living in the orphanage—children who owned nothing and had no one.

How dare she feel restless and unhappy when she owned several homes, had dozens of servants, hardly ever wore the same elegant outfit twice, ate fresh gourmet food for every meal, attended elaborate parties and social events, and could purchase anything she wanted?

She had everything . . . except the one thing that mattered most. Freedom.

With her chest tightening, she peeked out of the closet again toward Bishop. He was still occupied with the book.

She reached for the two letters in Constance's hands—one from each of the men. Even though the closet was shadowed, she could distinguish the bold print of the Colorado rancher.

Constance had first seen the rancher's advertisement in late June, and she'd written him a letter. However, when she hadn't heard back, she'd also corresponded with the man from Kansas.

The Kansas stockman had responded promptly, letting Constance know that he was a widower with two young children. He not only wanted a mother for his children but was also interested in having a large family and longed for a companion who would make a happy, pleasant home for his family.

Constance had decided to accept the stockman's proposal and had had a letter ready to send to him when she'd finally heard back from the Colorado rancher last week. The rancher had let her know he liked her qualifications and wanted her to travel west to become his wife.

Now Constance had two marriage proposals and didn't know how to choose the right one.

Of course, there were many reasons why answering a matrimonial ad was a risky affair. Tales abounded of both brides and grooms presenting themselves falsely in such advertisements and letters, crossing the country to meet each other only to find someone completely unsuitable with bad habits, uncouth behavior, and disagreeable temperaments. There were even stories about thievery, adultery, and murder.

But Constance had pointed out that even when

meeting a man locally, she might not really be able to assess his true character, at least not entirely.

Genevieve only had to think of her stepmother to know the truth of that. Lenora had hidden her true qualities until well after Papa had married her. Genevieve had been fifteen at the time, and Lenora had fooled even her in those early days.

Were Constance's two potential husbands playacting too? Or were they being genuine?

Genevieve opened the Colorado rancher's letter first.

She'd already read the few brief paragraphs during her previous visit to the orphanage last week. Quite honestly, she didn't need to look again. The words had lingered in her mind ever since.

The rancher had been honest about his wife running away with another man and asking for a divorce. The woman hadn't wanted their baby and had left him to raise the child alone on his cattle ranch.

After experiencing the heartache of the rejection, he'd explained, he would prefer to keep a new marriage platonic and was seeking a mother for his baby.

At least he was honest about his intentions.

Genevieve found one of the last lines of his letter: *"I'm looking for a partnership. I'll provide for you, and I won't expect anything of you in return except for you to be a good mother to my little fellow. I promise you'll have complete freedom from the usual demands."*

Genevieve flushed inwardly, as she had the last time she'd read it. Although she was innocent of the ways between men and women, she knew he was referring to the marriage bed.

Even so, the phrases *I won't expect anything of you* and *complete freedom* resonated down to her soul again today as much as before. Even if she was taking the words slightly out of context, her gaze locked on them as if they were the very sustenance she needed.

What would her life be like without expectations? With complete freedom?

The urge to have that kind of existence swelled so swiftly and strongly that she had the overwhelming need to take the rancher's letter and reply to it herself. But this wasn't her letter to respond to. It was Constance's.

Constance had been whispering about the pros and cons of both men, and Genevieve hadn't heard a word she'd said. Now the young woman paused and watched Genevieve with expectant eyes, still waiting for her to give an opinion on which man to marry.

Genevieve handed back the letters. "I do believe the Kansas stockman will make you happier."

"You do?"

"The rancher sounds wounded, emotionally closed off, and less willing to have a normal future. The stockman presents himself as though he is ready to move forward and find happiness again."

Constance was nodding, agreeing as usual, as if she'd never heard wiser counsel. "The rancher only wants a mother for his little tyke, but the stockman wants a wife."

"Such an arrangement would be ideal for me, but not for you."

Constance's brows lifted. "Ideal for you?"

"I shouldn't have said anything . . ."

Constance snapped her fingers. "You're the solution to my problem."

"What problem?"

"I don't want to disappoint either man by having to turn down one of the proposals."

Genevieve was embarrassed to admit just how much over the past week she'd thought about answering a matrimonial advertisement of her own to escape from Lenora's control.

If only Lenora hadn't been appointed as her guardian after Papa died four years ago. But without any other living relatives, he'd made Lenora the caretaker, had believed she would be a kind and loving stepmother. Genevieve had hoped so too, but Lenora had become increasingly overbearing and controlling, especially after all that had happened with Prescott Price last year.

Of course, Lenora had claimed she was just trying to protect America's wealthiest heiress from the many swindlers who wanted to take advantage of her. But Genevieve had known neither Prescott nor his father had been guilty of anything Lenora had perpetrated.

Since then, Lenora had not only taken control over Genevieve's suitors but also begun to determine how Genevieve could spend her time, what she should wear, and what friends she could socialize with.

Over recent months, Genevieve had felt as if a noose were being drawn tighter around her neck, threatening to strangle the life out of her. She often reminded herself she only had to endure one more year until she turned twenty-one. Then her stepmother's guardianship would come to an end, and Genevieve would have full access to her inheritance and finally regain control of her life.

But how would she be able to persevere for twelve more months when each day had become unbearable?

The only bright spots in her week were her visits to the orphanage. Lenora had already cut off Genevieve's involvement in the other charities she loved, claiming that they were taking advantage of her. But her stepmother hadn't prevented the twice-a-week visits to Open Door since the work mostly involved holding babies. What fault could be found with that?

Whatever the case, Constance's suggestion to marry the Colorado rancher was more than a little appealing. In fact, Genevieve's mind raced with the possibilities. She could hide there in the remote location, take care of his baby, and then file for an annulment next spring when she turned twenty-one and was no longer under Lenora's guardianship.

Obviously, she wouldn't want to inconvenience the rancher. But since he'd made it clear he was remarrying to provide a caretaker for his child, she could hire a nursemaid to take her place when it was time to depart. The rancher probably couldn't afford to hire help, or he would have done it instead of considering marriage. But she could easily pay for such a service.

Constance was sizing Genevieve up. "We're similar enough that I think you could take my place."

"And pretend to be you?" Genevieve couldn't believe she was actually considering Constance's suggestion.

"I didn't tell him too much. I described my appearance, told him about having grown up an orphan, and explained my duties here at Open Door."

"What happens when I arrive and have blue eyes instead of brown?"

Constance waved a hand as though it didn't matter. "He probably won't remember what color I mentioned."

"And the fact that I did not grow up an orphan?"

"Your parents are both gone. That makes you an orphan, doesn't it?"

"I don't know, Constance . . ." It seemed deceptive.

"What's one woman over another? He won't care as long as you're devoted to his baby. That's all that matters to him."

Could she really give up everything for a year? Would it be worth it in order to have freedom?

"Well?" Constance's expression held anticipation.

"I should just find myself a husband here in the city." But even as she said the words, after all that had happened with Prescott, she never wanted to put another man in danger of Lenora's scheming.

At a throat clearing in the hallway just outside the closet, Genevieve stiffened. She didn't have to turn to know that Bishop was behind her. How much of her conversation with Constance had he overheard?

Instead of turning, she bent and picked up a recently donated item of baby clothing from a crate on the floor. She folded it and placed it with other similar-sized clothing on the shelf. Constance followed suit.

After several moments of silence while she and Constance folded more clothing, Bishop cleared his throat again. "Miss Hollis?"

"What is it, Bishop?" She placed a tiny shirt on the shelf.

"Mrs. Hollis has instructed me to bring you home after an hour." His voice held a note of regret.

She wanted to protest and tell Bishop that she was staying for the full two hours. But she also knew if she didn't go home with him on time, Lenora would fire him from his position and make it difficult for him to get another job in New York City.

Genevieve had learned Lenora's tactics from past disobediences. While Lenora couldn't specifically punish

Genevieve, she did punish others because she knew all too well that Genevieve had a soft heart and couldn't abide letting others suffer.

Genevieve began to slowly fold one last item of clothing. "Am I only going to be allowed one hour from now on, Bishop?"

The driver hesitated. "I'm afraid Mrs. Hollis has decided this is to be your last visit at the orphanage."

"What?" Genevieve spun, and in the process, knocked a stack of clothing off the shelf so that the adorable outfits fluttered in disarray over the closet floor.

Bishop was gripping the Mark Twain book tightly, his silver brows furrowed with dismay. "I'm sorry, Miss Hollis. I truly am."

Genevieve's mind raced with a hundred thoughts. Why was Lenora doing this? Why now? What harm was there in letting her volunteer at the orphanage? How could she take away something so worthwhile?

Genevieve's spine turned rigid with all the objection coursing through her body. But as with everything else, she had no power, no voice, no freedom. She had to do as Lenora dictated or bring harm to Bishop or someone else, possibly even Constance.

She met the young woman's gaze.

Constance's eyes were wide with questions. It was almost as if she was insinuating that without the orphanage work, what else was there? Why not take the

Colorado rancher's invitation to be his baby's mother?

Genevieve agreed. What was tying her to New York City? She had no reason to stay. According to the rancher, if she went to Colorado, she'd have independence, few expectations, and freedom. How could she say no to that, especially now?

She gave a curt nod to her friend, hoping to communicate that she was agreeable to the plan. "I hope to convince my stepmother to allow me at least one more visit. But just in case I cannot sway her, I shall say goodbye now."

"I'll be here until the end of the week."

They had so much more they needed to discuss, but they'd run out of time.

Genevieve wrapped her arms around Constance in a hug and then leaned against her ear. "I'll do it."

As Genevieve broke away, Constance slipped one of the letters into her hand. Genevieve folded it, shoved it into her skirt pocket, and prayed she could truly escape from her stepmother's clutches and find her way to the rancher.

2

Hopefully, today he'd finally have a letter from New York City.

Ryder Oakley situated his son more securely in the makeshift sling Clementine had sewn for him. Then he swung open the door to Worth's General Store.

As the waft of spices and fresh produce greeted him, so did silence.

A sweeping glance around the other customers told Ryder all he needed to know. Everyone was staring at him as usual, the same way they'd been doing since back in February, when Sadie had told everyone she was carrying his child. Of course, the day after he'd discovered she was pregnant, he'd married her and, not long after, built her a house on a homestead near Frisco, north of his family's ranch.

If only that had been the end of the scandal. But no, it had just been the beginning. Sadie had quickly gotten tired of married life and being so far from town. She'd left him, found another man, then asked for a divorce.

Now everyone in Summit County, Colorado, knew he was a divorced single father with an infant he was taking care of while at the same time eking out an existence for himself on his new ranch. To make matters worse, they also knew he'd sent away for a mail-order bride . . . and that he was waiting to hear back from the woman he'd corresponded with.

As much as he wanted to ignore the stares, he couldn't. He threw out a scowl and then started through the store toward the back and the faded curtain that separated the store from the telegram and post office.

Floor-to-ceiling shelves lined every wall of the elongated store and overflowed with every imaginable item a person could need and then some. He passed by his sister Clementine's candy on top of and inside a glass shelving unit—everything from chocolates to hard candies, although she didn't have as much for sale anymore. And it was his fault.

He stifled a growl of frustration at himself for how much he'd inconvenienced his sister over the summer. Clem had never once complained about riding up to his place several days a week to stay with him and help watch Boone, but Ryder had noticed the strain in her face from time to time.

As loving and helpful as Clementine always was, he

felt bad about imposing upon her.

And he was tired of having to rely on other people. He wanted to be independent and handle everything on his own, including the baby. But the fact was, Boone was a lot more work than he'd ever anticipated.

Now at ten weeks old, the little fellow was sleeping better at night and taking longer naps during the day. He didn't seem quite so breakable and delicate anymore either. He was becoming more alert and noticing what was going on around him. And over the past week, he'd started smiling—real big smiles that tugged at Ryder's heart.

Ryder patted the underside of the sling, feeling the weight of his son's body curled up against him. He glanced down to find that Boone was peering up at him with dark-brown eyes very much like his own, his smattering of woodsy brown hair also the same color as Ryder's.

At times, he could see Sadie in the shape of the boy's eyes and in his chin. But most of the time, Ryder saw a miniature version of himself: a refined nose, wide forehead, and strongly chiseled jaw—not that anyone could see Ryder's jaw with the short beard that covered it.

Ryder tipped up the brim of his Stetson to get a better view of the baby.

Mr. Worth stepped through a curtained-off hallway at the back of the store, rolling up the sleeves of his white dress shirt, which was covered by a navy vest and topped off with a bow tie. Hatless, his dark brown hair was clipped short, and his beard was neatly trimmed. "How's baby Boone today?"

"Getting big." Ryder liked the storekeeper, which was more than he could say for most people in town.

A stocky, middle-aged man, Mr. Worth had a youthful look about his features. Maybe it was the lack of wrinkles. Maybe it was the friendliness of his eyes. Or maybe it was the warmth in the man's smile. Whatever it was, the fellow made the awkward venture inside the store more tolerable.

Ryder stopped at the back counter and tapped it absently, then dropped his voice. "Came to see if I have any mail."

Thankfully, most of the customers were no longer staring at him and had returned to their shopping. Or at least, they were pretending to browse, probably hoping to pick up more gossip about him.

Mr. Worth shook his head. "Sorry, son, but I don't have anything for you yet."

Disappointment reared up inside of Ryder even more keenly than during his visit to town last week. Maybe Constance Franklin from New York City wasn't planning to come after all. Of the several inquiries he'd received, he'd liked hers the best. Probably because she was an orphan like he was. And because she worked at an orphanage and loved children.

He'd gotten a letter from her initially, letting him know of her interest in the advertisement. That had been in late June. He'd written back, giving her more details about his situation and about Boone, but he hadn't heard from her since then. Now it was already early August.

What if his honesty about being divorced had scared her away? Maybe reputable women didn't want to be linked to a divorced man.

"Sure wish I had better news for you." Mr. Worth had swiped a rag and was wiping down the counter in front of him.

"It's all right. I'm getting along just fine." Ryder tried to project confidence into his voice so that no one would doubt him. Because most of the time, he *was* getting along without a woman.

He'd had a lot to learn about babies and bottles and burping. He could change diapers and give Boone a bath and settle him down when he was crying.

Yet, for as much as he was surviving, he couldn't deny that his life would be easier if he had a helpmate. Besides, he wanted Boone to have both a mother and a father— something he'd lacked until the Oakleys had adopted him when he'd been eleven and his brother Tanner had been nine.

He didn't like to think of the portion of his life before he'd met the Oakleys. Those years were a blur of being in and out of orphanages and homes, trying to survive and take care of Tanner and not be separated from him. Then when he'd turned eleven and learned he'd have to go to an industrial school and leave Tanner behind, that's when he'd finally decided they would run away to the West.

They'd gotten to Independence by steamboat and then stowed away in a supply wagon leaving on the Oregon Trail. They'd ridden for several days before being caught. Of course, they'd been too far along to be sent back to Independence. But they'd also become a burden on the families who were a part of the caravan, all of whom had brought enough food and supplies for their families and didn't have extra for two growing boys.

Except the Oakleys. Boone Oakley and his wife Hannah had welcomed him and Tanner into their family and treated them like sons. They'd shared everything they had, including all their love and affection. When they'd arrived in Colorado, Boone had asked him and Tanner to stay.

Ryder had wanted that more than anything, and so had Tanner. And everyone in the Oakley family had been excited when they'd agreed to join in the new adventure of establishing a horse ranch. Less than six months later, it had seemed only natural to become a part of their family officially through adoption.

Now fourteen years later, Ryder could hardly remember life without being in the Oakley family—or at least, he didn't like thinking about what life had been like before that. And he'd come to love his adoptive pa so deeply that he'd named his son after him.

Unfortunately, the past months had been hard, starting with the death of his adoptive pa in January. Shortly after that, he and Tanner had gotten into an enormous fight. They hadn't resolved the conflict, and so there was a lot of tension whenever they were together. Then he'd made a mess of things with Sadie and his marriage. And to top it all, his adoptive ma had died in May.

Ryder blew out a tense breath just thinking about all he'd experienced over the past year—more trouble than he'd had in a long time. So much so, the nightmares had started up again—nightmares he hadn't had in years. In fact, just thinking about the nightmares made his skin prickle.

At the tiny wail-like grunt from the sling, Ryder patted his son. Then he placed his weekly list down on the counter for the usual baby formula and food staples. "I'd be obliged if you'd add these items to my tab."

Mr. Worth picked up the sheet, but before he could answer, his eyes narrowed on a newcomer entering the store. "Uh-oh."

Ryder glanced over his shoulder to the sight of Sadie on the arm of her husband, the owner of the Wild Whiskey Saloon, Axe Lyman. Against his white trousers and white vest, the shiny gold of all his buttons stood out, as did the crimson rose he wore in his lapel. His long hair was slicked back with so much pomade it looked wet. Though his face was freshly groomed and smooth, it contained a haggardness that never went away and a hardness that likely came from dealing with the drunks and riffraff who frequented his saloon.

Uh-oh was right. Last time Ryder had come across Axe and Sadie, Axe had been itching for a fight and had thrown a punch at Ryder—had even threatened to kill him if he ever came around Sadie again.

Sadie was gussied up in what looked like a fancy new gown, and her fair hair was piled on top of her head in curls. She was a fine-looking woman, there was no arguing that.

But Axe didn't need to worry about him wanting Sadie back. There was more chance of a rattler growing butterfly wings than of him ever wishing to have Sadie as his wife again.

He could admit he'd always struggled with his lust over women. And he wasn't proud of his waywardness now that he'd matured and had a baby as a result. He honestly wasn't sure why women liked him, since he was gruff and silent and didn't lead them on. Maybe they relished the challenge of trying to win him.

Whatever it was, Sadie had approached him last year and made it clear she was interested. He hadn't been all that enamored with her and shouldn't have spent time in her bed.

At twenty-five, he hadn't been aiming to get married, hadn't wanted a baby or a wife or a family. He'd figured he'd work at High Country Ranch as a cowboy until he was old and limping around with bowlegs.

But when he'd found out Sadie was expecting his baby, he'd done what his adoptive pa would have wanted him to do to fix the situation. He'd asked her to marry him.

"Well, if it ain't the baby daddy himself." Axe's slow southern drawl filled the silence of the store.

"Come on now, Axe." Sadie's retort was as sassy as always. "He's a fine daddy, and you shouldn't be making fun of him." She fixed her big blue eyes upon Ryder, as though waiting for him to thank her for coming to his defense.

He didn't need her defense, though. Didn't even want it. Didn't want anything from her except to leave him alone to raise their child peacefully. A part of him worried that she might change her mind and want Boone back. And if that happened, what if he was forced to relinquish his son to her?

As irrational and unfounded as the fear was, it was another reason he'd taken Clementine's advice to place the advertisements in the newspapers in Denver, Chicago, and New York City. With a wife for himself and mother for his son, he hoped no one would question his right to have Boone.

Axe snorted. "Can't help it if Ryder looks like a woman with the way he carries that baby around."

Ryder also didn't want any more altercations with Axe calling into question his ability to be a good father. He tipped the brim of his hat at Mr. Worth, who was still watching Axe and Sadie with narrowed eyes. "I'll come back for my supplies later."

The store owner gave him a nod, as though he approved of the decision to avoid a fight. "I'll have Grady ride your supplies out to High C to Clementine so she can bring them with her when she helps you this week."

"Much obliged." Ryder tapped the counter and then forced himself to put one foot in front of the other as he headed toward the door. Every eye followed him, but he tried to act again as if he didn't care about the judgment. Or the curiosity. No doubt half the customers were hoping for a fight between him and Axe.

He wasn't about to give them what they were waiting for and avoided looking at both Sadie and Axe, still standing near the door.

"Go on and run," Axe taunted as he stalked past. "You oughta be scared of me."

Ryder's step hitched with the need to halt and prove he wasn't scared of the fellow. But that was exactly what Axe wanted—to provoke him. Ryder tossed the door open and stepped out as empty-handed as he'd been when he'd entered.

And he was still no closer to having the help he needed. It felt a thousand miles away.

3

Today was the day.

Genevieve paused in the doorway of the parlor, clasping her hands together to keep them from trembling.

Shortly after moving in, Lenora had hired one of the best interior designers in New York City to renovate the house. Even at midmorning, with the August sunshine streaming in from the tall front windows, every lantern in the room was lit because Lenora wanted to make sure each piece of polished furniture gleamed and every gilded decoration glinted.

Perched on the edge of a settee across from Mr. Morgan, their lawyer, Lenora was attired in a new garnet silk dress. Her brown hair was styled in a high updo with short curly bangs framing an elegant face that was only just beginning to show her forty years.

At the sight of Genevieve, her conversation came to an abrupt halt, and she stood, surveying Genevieve as she usually did to make sure she was the picture of perfection.

Mr. Morgan, not only their family lawyer but also a longstanding friend of Papa's, rose too. "Nice to see you, Genevieve." The perfect gentleman, he wore a wool frock coat over a matching vest and trousers, and a white cravat accented with a gold stick pin. He'd shed his tall hat, and his dark hair gleamed with hints of silver.

Genevieve forced herself to smile congenially at both Lenora and Mr. Morgan—or at least, she hoped it was calm and pleasant and didn't betray her nervousness. "I'm leaving for the dress fitting." It was the weekly appointment Lenora made for her so that she was continually supplied with new gowns in order to maintain their reputation as the most fashionably attired women in New York City.

The narrow skirt of her plum silk-and-taffeta day dress made movement more difficult and wasn't ideal for what she had planned for the morning. But Lenora had chosen the gown along with the matching short-brimmed, boxy hat now tilted precariously at the top of Genevieve's head over the tight ringlets of hair flowing from the waterfall style.

Lenora scanned her a moment longer before nodding. Then her attention latched on to the black velvet chatelaine attached at Genevieve's waist with a brooch pin. Genevieve had been hoping that Lenora wouldn't notice the different purse, but she should have known her stepmother wouldn't miss that detail. Lenora never missed any details.

The woman frowned and started to cross toward her. "Why aren't you using the matching chatelaine?"

"I spilled coffee on it." Intentionally.

Halting in the center of the room, Lenora released an exasperated sigh. Then she examined Genevieve again from her hat down to her boots.

Genevieve held her breath, praying her stepmother wouldn't notice the way the bag was bulging more than usual.

After several more long seconds of scrutiny, Lenora waved a hand at Genevieve. "Fine. It'll have to do."

The wave was all the dismissal Genevieve needed. She nodded demurely, then she turned back into the entry hallway and stepped across the marble tile as rapidly as her tight skirt would allow, wanting to get out of the house before Lenora called her back.

Once Genevieve was seated in the Victoria carriage and on her way to the dress shop, she finally allowed herself a full breath. Even though the top was down and she was on display to the city as usual, the way Lenora wanted, Genevieve had accomplished step one of her escape plan—exiting the house without Lenora stopping her.

Step two—evading Bishop at the dress shop—would be more difficult. But after debating all the options over the past three days since saying goodbye to Constance at the orphanage, she'd decided the dress fitting at Madame Moreau's would allow her the best chance of slipping away from Bishop.

Genevieve pressed a hand against her chatelaine and felt the outline of the jewelry she'd placed there. Lenora didn't allow her to have any cash or coins, probably to keep her dependent as much as possible.

So yesterday, during her outing to the milliner's, she'd had Bishop stop by one of her favorite jewelers. Thankfully, he'd waited outside instead of accompanying her into the store.

The reprieve had allowed her to ask the jeweler if he'd be willing to purchase a ring and necklace from her. Of course, the older gentleman had nodded at her explanation that she was trying to downsize her collection and tactfully referenced the rumors that she was selling family assets.

She'd merely nodded and taken his offer for the elegant pieces, which had been higher than she'd hoped for—enough that she could easily pay for the expenses she was sure to encounter while traveling in the days ahead.

She'd concealed the bank notes in her chemise until she'd been able to tuck them away into her chatelaine along with as much jewelry as she could fit. She'd only had a few seconds to do so while the maid had been making the bed and had her back turned to the dressing table.

Genevieve pressed a hand to the drawstring purse again and whispered another silent prayer that the next part of her escape would go as smoothly as the first.

The dress shop was busy when she arrived, but as the best-paying and most frequent customer, she always received preferential treatment from Madame Moreau. It wasn't long before Genevieve was at the back of the shop in the most spacious dressing room—the one closest to the rear door of the establishment. It was also an area off-limits to Bishop.

Genevieve sat in the plush chair while the head seamstress brought in and hung up the two newest gowns that needed alterations.

Finally, the woman turned to her and smiled warmly—an invitation to stand and let her assist in taking off her garments.

Genevieve glanced at the corner chamber pot and pretended to be embarrassed. "Would you mind terribly if I undress myself today?" Since the buttons were at the front of her bodice, the task would be manageable—if she were actually intending to do it.

The seamstress kept her eyes averted from the chamber pot. "Of course, Miss Hollis."

"In fact, why don't you finish with your other customer first."

"Oh, it's no trouble. One of the other seamstresses will assist her."

"Please. I don't mind waiting."

The woman hesitated, then nodded. "Very well." She left reluctantly, likely fearing she would get in trouble from Madame Moreau for attending to another customer instead of their prized patron. With such reluctance, the seamstress would be back sooner rather than later. That meant the chance of escaping was much too limited. That also meant Genevieve couldn't waste a single second.

As soon as the woman disappeared and the curtain fell into place, Genevieve rose, crossed toward the back door, and let herself out as soundlessly as possible.

The narrow alleyway she found herself in was shadowed by the tall buildings on either side and deserted except for two small children a dozen paces away, kicking a ball. At the sight of her, they halted and stared with wide eyes, likely wondering what a fine lady like herself was doing there.

What exactly was she doing? Could she really run away and marry a complete stranger? What if in doing so, she found herself in a worse situation altogether? Would she be safer staying and trying to endure one more year?

Even as the thought flashed through her mind, she shook her head. Lenora had taken away the only activity giving her any hope. Without her visits to the orphanage and without anything to do, she would go mad.

Besides, she'd already decided that if living with the Colorado rancher didn't work the way she hoped, she didn't have to stay. She could sneak away from him just as she was from Lenora.

However, if he was as kindhearted as he'd sounded in his letter, the one Constance had given to her that contained his address, then she would be fine. She'd help him for a year, and in doing so, he'd help her.

She braced her shoulders, then began walking down the alley, away from the dress shop. She'd already planned to go at least two blocks before heading out to the main thoroughfare and boarding the streetcar that would take her to the train station. The trouble was that she had to get on the streetcar before Bishop realized she was gone from the shop.

With her heart thudding ominously, she picked up her pace as best she could with her tight skirt. She expected the back door of the dress shop to barge open at any moment for the head seamstress to call after her. But as she reached the second cross street and began to turn, she glanced back to see that not only was the door of the shop still closed, but the two children had raced away and were no longer there to report her whereabouts to anyone who might come out to search for her.

As she hastened to the corner where the horse-drawn streetcar made its stop, she kept in the shadows of the closest building, one eye on her Victoria carriage still parked in front of Madame Moreau's shop down the street.

Thankfully, the streetcar was already within sight. When the large conveyance pulled to a stop, she tried to hide behind the others who were getting on. But it wasn't until she was seated and the horses started up again that she took a deep breath.

Had she actually done it? Made her escape from Bishop?

She guessed she'd been gone from the shop for approximately ten minutes, which meant Bishop and others would begin hunting for her before too long.

As the streetcar rolled farther down the steel tracks at the center of the road, she kept waiting for Bishop to race after the conveyance and shout at the driver to stop. But when long minutes passed without any interference, she allowed herself to hope that maybe she could make it to the train depot and part three of her plan.

After changing streetcars two more times, she finally arrived at Grand Central Depot. The station was just as busy as it had been the last time she'd ridden a train with Lenora—the previous winter, when they'd traveled to Florida.

As she made her way inside to the ticket counters, she wished she blended into the crowds better. She knew she was leaving a bright trail in her wake—that a fashionable gentlewoman like her was sure to draw the attention of the staff and other passengers alike.

As part of step three, she bought a ticket south on the

Atlantic Coast Line, hoping that anyone looking for her would believe she was on her way to Florida to the resort where she usually stayed. However, when she reached New Jersey or thereabouts, she would make a switch to another line heading west.

Before doing that, she'd find a store to purchase a valise, clothing, and any other supplies she might need. She'd change into the simpler garb, something that would make her less noticeable. Hopefully after that, anyone who might be tracking her would lose her trail.

If all went well, she'd be able to move into step four of her runaway plan, which involved riding the transcontinental railroad west and arriving in Denver in less than a week. After that, she'd have to find a way to get up into the mountains.

As she settled onto her seat and other passengers bustled around her, she slipped the letter from the Colorado rancher from her pocket and unfolded it. She hadn't dared read it since the closet at the orphanage with Constance earlier in the week. She'd wanted to keep it hidden from the servants because many of them reported back to Lenora.

Now, as she waited for the train to depart, she smoothed the letter out in her lap, taking in the bold print. She read the few short paragraphs again. His words were direct and no-nonsense. He also sounded like a dedicated father who wanted the best for his baby—so much so that he was willing to get remarried even though he didn't particularly want to.

Although the letter didn't provide much information, she felt as though she was getting to know him just a little, enough that she could tell he was a good, solid man who would treat her with respect. And hopefully allow her to be independent and free.

She drew her finger across his name at the end of the letter. Ryder Oakley. "I'm on my way, Ryder Oakley," she whispered.

The real question was, what he would say when he discovered she wasn't Constance Franklin? Would he still want her? Or should she do as Constance had suggested and pretend to be her?

A burst of the steam whistle filled the air, startling her. A second later, the wheels clacked against the track, and the train began to creep forward.

She folded up the letter and glanced out the window, which was open to generate a breeze through the stuffy compartment. Through the people milling about the platform, a man with silver hair and wearing a dark suit caught her attention. Bishop.

He was near the door of the depot and was frantically scanning the people.

With her heart picking up tempo, she flattened herself against the seat, hoping he wouldn't be able to see her through the train window.

How had he traced her to the depot so quickly?

The train car creaked as the speed increased, and the platform fell behind, away from sight. But she didn't sit forward, holding herself motionless and praying he wouldn't figure out which train she was on but all the while suspecting he wouldn't be far behind.

4

Genevieve felt as if she were being followed.

As she stepped down from the stagecoach in Frisco, Colorado, she couldn't keep from glancing around at the dozen or so buildings that made up the town, expecting to find Bishop or some other man waiting for her, ready to grab her and haul her back home.

Not that she'd seen Bishop since the train depot in New York City a week ago. If he'd trailed her, she'd obviously kept one step ahead of him. She'd made the train switch in New Jersey and had foregone the shopping for necessities that she'd originally anticipated. In fact, she hadn't stopped at all until she'd reached Independence, Missouri, hoping to put as much distance as possible between herself and anyone searching for her.

Finally, in Independence, she'd taken a day to purchase everything she needed for the remainder of her trip, including a large valise of clothing and shoes and toiletries. Though the frontier town had been much smaller than New York City, the business district had been plentiful, filled with stores selling every kind of ware a person could want or need.

The ready-made skirts and bodices had been much simpler than anything she'd ever worn, but they'd been more comfortable than the tight, plum-colored gown she'd traveled in for several days. She'd also shed her corset in favor of the lightweight chemise she was currently wearing underneath her bodice.

Already she felt freer. Free from her stifling apparel. Free from hovering servants. And free from Lenora's control. The tight, heavy shackles had fallen away.

And she was proud of herself for outsmarting Lenora and making it all the way to Colorado by herself without any help. Perhaps she had more strength inside herself than she realized.

As she stepped away from the stagecoach onto the dirt road that ran the length of the town, she took in another deep breath of the fresh mountain air, just as she'd done at every stop. She couldn't get enough of the crisp, clean air, so different than the stale, humid air that permeated New York City in August.

She tipped up the brim of the straw hat she'd purchased in Independence and let the high-altitude sun bathe her face as she feasted upon the scenery—the rugged mountains rising all around.

At midafternoon, the town, with a mixture of log structures and weathered gray clapboard buildings, appeared sleepy. A tumbleweed blowing on the street was the only sign of life. A loose shutter on a nearby building creaked in the breeze and was the only sound. It was the smallest and most rugged town she'd visited yet.

The stagecoach driver, in the process of unstrapping her bag from among the luggage still on the top, paused and cocked his head toward the building across the street. "You want your bag delivered to the hotel?"

It was a simple two-story building with the words "Frisco Inn" painted on a board over the door.

"Actually," she said, tucking a loose wisp of hair behind her ear, "I need to hire a driver. Do you know where I could hire such a service?"

"Sure do," called an older fellow standing behind her in the open door of a barn with chipped and peeling paint visible in patches here and there.

Although she hadn't asked her question of the older fellow, she directed her attention his way. He stood below a sign reading "Livery." He was coatless and hatless, his trousers stained, and his once-white shirt a dirty shade of gray. He spat out a glob of tobacco, then wiped his sleeve across his beard and mouth, revealing blackened teeth. "I can get you any place you need to go. The name's Virgil."

The stagecoach driver hopped down with her valise.

"That all the luggage you got?" Virgil's wiry brows rose.

"Yes, it is." She took her valise from the driver, a coating of dust now covering the once-spotless floral print brocade. The bag was heavy with all she'd purchased, but she'd hefted it around for the past few days without the aid of a servant, and she was growing accustomed to the task.

"Then we'll go by horseback," Virgil declared in a decisive tone. "The roads around here ain't too wagon-friendly."

As a single woman without a chaperone, she was already at a disadvantage, drawing people who wanted to prey upon her. It had been especially true when she'd been wearing her fancy gown. Even attired in unpretentious garments, she probably still appeared naïve and inexperienced.

But she'd traveled enough with her papa, both in the United States and Europe, to gain a sense about people, quickly assessing whom she could trust. Although Virgil was as weathered and worn as his livery barn, his expression contained a forthrightness that told her he was a decent man.

He spat again into the dirt. "You can ride, can't you?"

"Of course." Her papa had made sure she'd learned how to ride, and she'd always enjoyed going to their summer home on Cape Cod and riding the beautiful Arabians her father kept there.

"Where you headed?" Virgil started into the barn.

She headed toward the wide door. "I need to go to Ryder Oakley's homestead."

The fellow popped back out of the barn so quickly she almost tripped in her haste to stop. Both of his brows arched high. "You're Ryder's mail-order bride?"

"Mail order?"

"Constance Franklin? The woman he sent away for?"

Oh dear. She'd wrestled all week with how to handle the situation once she arrived—whether to explain her real identity or to take Constance's. A part of her had decided that honesty was the best option. She didn't want to deceive Ryder Oakley into thinking she was someone she was not.

On the other hand, she'd seen a newspaper two days ago that a gentleman had left on the seat in the train car. One of the front-page articles had been about her, the country's wealthiest heiress who was missing. She hadn't been able to read the entire article, but she'd skimmed far enough to see that it described her in detail and that there was a reward for information about her.

She'd made sure after that to tuck her dark hair out of sight and keep the brim of her hat low to hide her eyes. Even so, she would likely be easy to track to Independence, maybe even beyond.

Hopefully after Denver, no one would realize she'd ridden into the mountains. But if she continued to use her given name, then Bishop, or whoever else Lenora hired, would find her in no time. And she had no doubt Lenora would hire investigators to track her.

Virgil's brows were still arched high as he waited for her response to his question about being Constance Franklin.

"Mm-hmm," she managed. "That's me." Even as the words came out, she had to force herself not to cringe at the lie. But what else could she do at this point if she wanted to stay hidden? Perhaps she would tell Ryder Oakley the truth after she'd had some time to ascertain whether or not he was trustworthy enough to keep her secret. But for now, she wouldn't be hurting anyone to use Constance's name, would she?

"It's about time. Ryder's been waiting."

"So, he's still expecting someone—me?"

"Reckon so."

She hoped so.

"Course," Virgil continued, "Ryder don't come up here to Frisco as much as he goes to Breckenridge, since we don't get much mail here."

The thought had crossed her mind that perhaps Ryder had exchanged letters with more than one woman, the same way Constance had corresponded with more than one man. Genevieve had known there was the possibility that when she arrived at his homestead, he might have selected a different bride. But there was only one way to find out, and that was to go visit him.

Within minutes, she and Virgil were both mounted and her valise strapped behind her. As they started down Main Street, a few faces peeked out of the dusty windows, but otherwise, no one seemed to show much interest in a lone woman riding out to possibly become Ryder Oakley's new wife.

Virgil led the way south along a river that cut its way through the valley between two sets of enormous mountain ranges running from north to south. The ranges were equally majestic, with only a smattering of snow on the rocky peaks above the tree line—snow likely left from the previous winter.

They traveled for a couple of miles before Virgil veered to the west, following another river, this one smaller. The way grew rockier and steeper before it leveled off into a grassy pasture that was perfect for grazing cattle.

"That's it," Virgil called to her while nodding at something ahead.

She surveyed the area, spotting a herd of cattle in the distance. Beyond the cattle, she glimpsed the sloping shingled roof of a log barn.

They only had to travel a short distance more before the rest of the homestead took shape. A log home—much smaller than the barn—sat amidst the long grass against a picturesque backdrop of pine-covered mountain slopes. A curl of smoke wafted from a stone chimney, but otherwise the place looked as silent and deserted as the town.

A pile of wood was stacked against the cabin and an axe was lodged into a stump. An overgrown garden grew on the other side of the cabin, and a few chickens strutted in the grass and wildflowers that surrounded the buildings.

Only when they'd ridden past the cattle and were almost upon the barn did a man finally step out of the wide barn doorway. From what she could tell, he met the description in the advertisement: *6 feet 2 inches tall and 180 pounds.* But he was decidedly more muscular than she'd anticipated—although, if he was wrangling cattle for a living, he'd have to be strong.

He wore a tan Stetson with a braid of horsehair. A black-and-gray flannel shirt stretched across his broad shoulders and his bulky biceps. He had a blanket-like covering across his front, but it did nothing to hide the breadth of his chest and the muscles there. His denim trousers highlighted long sturdy legs, and tall leather boots with spurs completed the ensemble.

Virgil called out, "Howdy. Got your bride."

Ryder dropped his hand from where it rested on the handle of a revolver holstered at his waist. Then he moved out from the lengthening shadows of the barn, tipped up the brim of his hat, and watched their approach with an intensity that Genevieve wasn't sure she liked.

As they finally reined in their horses, Genevieve

couldn't stop herself from taking him in with as much scrutiny as he was her. Strands of brown hair curled up at his collar. His face was tan and covered in a layer of scruff and a short beard. He had a narrow nose, a strong, unsmiling mouth, and a fine forehead that was wreathed with wrinkles.

She tried to see past the scragginess, and imagined he would have a distinct jaw and chin and cheekbones once he was shaven. No doubt he would clean up well and look very fine. But at the moment, he had an air of ruggedness that left her no doubt he was a cowboy through and through.

At the wiggling of the blanket-like covering, his gaze dropped away from her to the bundle, and he patted it gently with large workworn hands.

Her attention shifted to the bundle now too. From the shape, she guessed the baby was strapped there to his chest to free up his hands for the many chores awaiting him every day. The hardness in his expression softened for a brief moment as he looked at his baby.

The one unguarded moment of gentleness was all she needed to reassure herself that Ryder was everything he'd claimed to be and that she didn't have to worry he'd misrepresented himself. It also helped that Virgil had spoken highly of Ryder and his whole family during the ride to the ranch. Although the wiry older man hadn't said much, it had been enough for her to conclude that the Oakley family was well-respected and well-liked.

When Virgil dismounted, she did too. After her feet landed on the ground, she waited for Ryder to say more—to introduce himself, to ask her something. But he was once again studying her, taking her in from her hat down to her skirt hem.

What did he think? Was he puzzling over who she was?

"Miss Franklin?" He finally lifted his gaze and met hers. The brown of his eyes was dark and rich and thick like a cup of hot chocolate. "I'm Ryder Oakley."

"I'm pleased to meet you."

Virgil spat a glob of tobacco, then cocked his head toward Genevieve. "Came on the stagecoach less than an hour ago."

Ryder was still scrutinizing her. Was he noticing discrepancies in her appearance already from what Constance had described in her letter?

At the nervous flutter in her stomach, she pressed her hand there.

He was watching her hand. "I was beginning to think you weren't interested. Or that maybe you didn't get my letter."

She tugged it out of her pocket. "I have it right here." The envelope was worn and creased now, but his handwriting was still visible.

His gaze flicked to it but then returned to her face.

She held her breath. Was he noticing that she had blue eyes instead of brown? Should she just admit she wasn't Constance after all? "Mr. Oakley—"

"You can call me Ryder."

"And you can call me Genevieve." The moment her real name slipped out, she cringed.

He studied her face more closely. "You don't go by Constance?"

Everything within her demanded that she tell him the truth. But after traveling all this way, she was weary and didn't want to chance that he might turn her away. At least, not at the moment. She didn't want to have to board another train or stagecoach. She didn't want to find a new place to go.

This ranch—she glanced around at the quiet fields that surrounded the barn and cabin—was secluded and far from anyone who would recognize her. She would easily be able to hide here.

She could feel both men now watching her and waiting for her answer. She curved her lips into a practiced smile. "I do prefer Genevieve."

They still didn't speak, clearly expecting additional enlightenment.

"It is my middle name and what my papa always called me." That was the truth, or at least a portion of it. Her papa had christened her Elizabeth after her mother, who had died during child birthing. But he'd never been able to make himself call her Elizabeth and had used her middle name, Genevieve, instead.

Finally, Ryder nodded. "Okay."

"Thank you." Maybe she'd been foolish to want to go by Genevieve. Maybe once people in the area learned of it, they'd make the connection to the missing heiress, Genevieve Hollis.

But at least she hadn't lied entirely about everything. And maybe using her given name would make her deception feel slightly less terrible.

5

His bride-to-be was here.

Ryder expelled a breath, releasing the tension that had been building with every passing day. Now almost a week after his last trip to Worth's General Store in Breckenridge to check for mail, when he'd run into Sadie and Axe, he'd just about given up hope and had almost decided to contact another of the women who'd written to him.

But here she was. Constance Franklin. Or Genevieve, as she preferred to be called.

From the tightness of her smile as she'd given the explanation for being called Genevieve, he guessed the story was more complicated than she'd revealed. But now wasn't the time or place to ask her about it.

Maybe there never would be a time and place. Maybe she'd never want to talk about her past with him. And that was okay, because he didn't want to talk about his either. Some things were too painful to discuss.

As Virgil silently untied her bag from behind the saddle, Ryder couldn't keep from studying her again. She wasn't what he'd expected. From the tone of her letter and the way she'd described herself, he'd pictured a sturdier and plainer woman, someone simple and down-to-earth.

But Genevieve . . . she was petite and stunning and held herself with a poise most women didn't have. Her skin was pale and perfect, like a pearl. Her hair was as dark as the thick bearskin rug Tanner had given him. Her face was elegant, with high cheekbones and full lips and a delicate nose.

And her eyes . . .

As though sensing his scrutiny, she lifted her long lashes to reveal a light blue, almost gray—the prettiest, most unique eye color he'd ever seen. She peered back at him directly, unabashedly, as if she had nothing to fear.

For a reason he didn't understand, his heart sped with a rhythm that was slightly erratic and too fast. Was he having a reaction to how beautiful she was? Because she wasn't intimidated by him? Or was he just relieved she'd arrived and now he wouldn't have to bear the burden of raising a child all on his own?

Whatever the case, he was having a difficult time comprehending the fact that this woman wanted to marry him. Surely someone so beautiful had a whole host of men who were interested in marrying her. So why had she decided to respond to his advertisement?

She'd mentioned that the orphanage where she was working would soon be reducing the number of staff and she would be unemployed, but surely there was more to her story than that.

When Virgil placed the bag by her feet, she tugged at the strings on her purse, which was pinned to her skirt. "Thank you, Virgil. I do appreciate your kind assistance." She withdrew a few bank notes.

Virgil reached out to take the cash but then hesitated and glanced at Ryder expectantly.

"I'll pay." Ryder stuck his hand into his trouser pocket and fumbled to find the loose change there.

She shoved the bills into Virgil's hand. "Please, allow me."

"No." Ryder pulled out two silver coins, not caring that his voice turned hard. "You already spent enough to get out here."

Virgil nodded vigorously at Ryder, as though agreeing with him, and was thrusting Genevieve's money back at her and taking Ryder's coins.

"I'd intended to wire you the funds for your trip." Ryder had been saving the little he had to help with the train and stagecoach.

"Thank you, Ryder." She tucked the bills back into her bag. "That is very considerate of you, but I assure you that paying for my trip to the West was not a hardship."

"It's my responsibility to take care of you now." He'd watched the way his adoptive pa had taken care of Ma, how he'd doted on her and rushed to meet her needs, even before she could voice them. He'd tried to follow Pa Oakley's example with Sadie, but she'd never given him or their marriage half a chance.

Regardless of the fact that he still wasn't all that eager for marriage, he intended to do the right thing by his new wife too. He'd take care of her, watch over her, and make sure she was happy.

Virgil was climbing back onto his mount while holding the reins of the horse Genevieve had ridden. As he settled into his saddle, he leveled a stern look at Ryder. "You'll be calling on the reverend soon?"

"Yep, real soon." Reverend Livingston lived in Breckenridge, which was about seven miles from his homestead. It was mostly a straight ride south along the Blue River, but it would still take him about an hour to get there. "Maybe tomorrow."

"Oh my." Genevieve ducked her head, light pink coloring her cheeks. "I regret I did not consider how inappropriate my staying here would be if we're not married."

Was it inappropriate? He shot a glance at Virgil, hoping the older man would know.

Virgil nodded as he situated himself in his saddle.

"Reckon you'll want to start things out right this time."

Ryder didn't have to ask what the older man meant. The scandal with Sadie was still alive and well. Boone was the living advertisement of it everywhere he went.

"Please forgive me for my thoughtlessness in coming out all this way." Genevieve picked up her bag and swiped up the lead line of the horse. "I will take a hotel room in town until we are wed."

"No, that won't be necessary." Now that he had her here, he had no intention of letting her go. What if she decided she hadn't liked what she'd seen, either of him or the ranch, then decided not to come back. "I'll go after the reverend right now."

She paused in her retreat. "I really do not mind residing in town for a few days."

He glanced to the position of the sun. "Still got plenty of time until nightfall."

She twisted at the handles of her bag. Maybe she was trying to find a nice way to say no to him and back out of the arrangement.

He took off his hat and jammed his fingers into his hair. What could he say or do to make her want to stay?

Boone gave another grunt, this time louder than the last.

Ryder bounced the baby and patted him, having learned over the past weeks what the different cries meant. This particular one meant Boone was hungry.

Ryder had been hoping to finish up the last of the shoeing, but Boone had already started fussing before Genevieve had arrived and now probably wouldn't be put off much longer.

Ryder pushed down the blanket to get a better view of the baby. His face was flushed, and his nose scrunched with another cry, louder than the last one.

"Sounds as if perhaps he's ready for a bottle?" Genevieve's tone was kind, and she was peering at Boone with a tender look in her eyes.

If he could get her interested in the baby, maybe she wouldn't leave. "Would you like to feed him while I go fetch the preacher?"

"I do not want to impose on you—"

"You'd be doing me a big favor by taking care of Boone for a while."

"Boone?" She finally released the lead line.

"I'm sure he'll take to you right away." Ryder untied the knot in the blanket at his shoulder. As the snug cocoon loosened, he held the baby and the blanket out to Genevieve.

She smiled down at Boone. "He's a darling. An absolute darling."

At the sound of her voice, Boone's grunts ceased, and he peered up at the beautiful woman as though he'd never seen anyone like her and could gaze at her all day.

"Go ahead." Ryder extended the baby even further.

"He may as well get acquainted with his new ma."

She hesitated only a moment longer before scooping Boone into her arms and cradling him against her chest as if she'd done that very thing hundreds of times in her life. She was clearly as experienced with children as she'd indicated. And fond of them too.

More tension eased from his shoulders. Someday, if they ever became comfortable around each other, he hoped to talk to her about her work in the orphanage and what that had been like, especially since she'd once been an orphan. But for now, it was enough to know that even if she wasn't exactly how he'd pictured her, she was already proving to be caring and good with children. And that was all that really mattered.

He thanked Virgil for bringing Genevieve out to the ranch, and then he stood awkwardly beside her, watching the older fellow ride away.

When the livery owner was no longer in sight, Genevieve turned her attention onto Boone, smiling at him and caressing his cheeks. "Are you ready to eat, little one?"

Ryder picked up her bag. "I'll show you where his bottles are, and then I'll be on my way."

"Thank you. That would be fine." She didn't take her eyes from Boone, was clearly more interested in the baby than in him. And that was okay too.

Ryder led the way through the tall grass to the one-room cabin that he'd been living in since his family had helped him build it earlier in the year. It wasn't a large place, but it had been big enough for him and Boone over the past months.

What would Genevieve think?

He hesitated in front of the door. "I'm planning to build a real house, hopefully next summer." Maybe by then he'd have enough saved up from the sale of his cattle to afford the lumber and supplies.

She'd angled her head and was studying the log construction. "So, this cabin is only a temporary living place?"

He nodded. Did her voice sound relieved, or was he imagining it? What if she hated living in the cabin out in the wilderness as much as Sadie had? What would he do then? What if she decided to leave him too? Maybe the problem was him and the simple fact that everyone he cared about eventually left him and always had.

No. He had to stop the whirlwind of his spiraling thoughts. If he didn't, he'd find himself in a bad place—a place he'd been in often enough to know it wasn't good for him or Boone.

He sucked in a fortifying breath, then pushed the door open to reveal the interior of the cabin. It wasn't fancy, but he'd done the best he could to make it homey. A full-sized bed took up one corner, covered with one of the colorful quilts Ma had made over the years. The makeshift cradle he'd built for Boone sat at the end of the bed, and a chest of drawers painted a bright blue stood beside the bed—a chest he'd purchased from a family moving farther west. At first, he'd considered repainting it, but the longer he had it in the cabin, the more he liked the color.

His family had given him an old table and chairs and sideboard they no longer used. And Tanner had given him the bearskin rug in front of the rocking chair. Over the weeks his sister Clementine had been coming to help him with Boone, she'd brought new things for his home with every visit—a tablecloth, doilies, curtains, pictures of Ma and Pa, and a wall-hanging that Ma had embroidered.

He'd added several shelves to the wall near the stove, and one contained the books he'd collected over the years, mostly gifts from his adopted family—some novels but mostly history books, because he loved any kind of history.

Even though he was satisfied with his new home, he tried to see it as Genevieve would, the way Sadie had when she'd first stepped into the cabin. She'd pivoted in a circle, and her eyes had rounded with disappointment. Would Genevieve do the same?

Genevieve entered behind him, and he didn't turn, didn't want to see any disappointment on her face. Instead, he approached the stove and tugged the kettle of water onto a front burner. Then he reached for a bottle on the shelf, along with the container of baby formula.

Genevieve's boots tapped on the plank floor as she crossed toward him. "I don't mind getting Boone's bottle ready."

As she stopped beside him, he paused and swallowed the rising anxiety. "If you'll be all right, then I'll head on out."

"I'll be all right." Her voice was gentle and reassuring.

He stood in front of the stove for several more heartbeats, wanting to say something else—something to reassure her that he'd be a good husband. But the words—as always—got stuck inside.

When she pried the bottle from his fingers, he finally stepped back. He was still too afraid to look at her face and gauge her reaction to his home, so he spun and stalked to the door. He halted halfway out. "I'll be back in a couple of hours."

"I'll be waiting." A spoon clinked against glass. She was already busy filling the bottle with the formula.

He had nothing to worry about. At least, that's what he tried to tell himself as he started toward the barn.

6

Genevieve was already in love with the mountains and the secluded ranch. And Boone was adorable.

She just wasn't quite sure what to think of Ryder.

Drawing in a breath of the thin, clean air, she let herself take in the scenery again, as she had dozens of times since arriving. From where she stood in the cabin door, she had a perfect view of the grassy fields that spread out to the eastern mountains. Had Ryder purposefully placed the cabin here so that he could admire the landscape every time he stepped out?

At a soft babble of baby noises, she turned back into the cabin and crossed to the cradle where she'd laid Boone for a nap shortly after he'd taken his bottle. So far during the hours that Ryder had been away, the baby had slept most of the time.

She'd taken advantage of the quiet to familiarize herself with the cabin and what supplies were available and had been surprised to find the sideboard well stocked with food, dishes, pots and pans, and cooking utensils. Although she'd never even stepped foot into the kitchens in her various homes, she'd learned a few basics in the kitchen at the orphanage, mainly about preparing bottles for the infants but also how to make hot cereal, soup, and stew.

During her exploration of the garden at the side of the cabin, she'd gathered enough vegetables—onions, carrots, green beans, a few potatoes, and herbs—and had made a simple soup, enjoying every moment of the freedom to create the meal.

Now that she'd had a taste of the independence she'd so desperately craved, she wasn't sure how she'd survived without it. Not only had she been able to wander around the cabin and garden and do whatever she pleased, but she'd had no one watching her every move, no one dictating what she needed to do next, no one criticizing how she looked or walked or held herself.

Even though she was weary from the past days of traveling, she felt invigorated and alive in a way she hadn't in a long time, probably since before her papa died. And she was also relieved that the situation had worked out the way it had. It truly appeared as though she'd found the perfect place to hide away from Lenora's reach for the next year. By the time she was near her twenty-first birthday, she'd probably be ready to return to civilization and the comforts of life.

But for now . . . she would relish the experience of living in this rugged land.

As she stooped to pick Boone up, he peered at her with the same brown eyes as his father. Except that Ryder's eyes were much more complicated and filled with sadness and worry and too many other emotions to name.

"How are you, little one?" She caressed Boone's soft cheek.

His eyes widened upon her as they had when he'd first met her, as though he hadn't quite expected to see her again.

"You'll get used to me." The moment she spoke the words, guilt pricked her conscience. The baby would likely grow attached to her over the coming months and assume she was his mother. How would he react when she left? Would it be difficult for him?

Of course, she still planned to hire a caregiver to take her place. But she hadn't considered how her leaving would impact Boone.

"Oh dear," she whispered as she let him grasp one of her fingers tightly in his fist. "I don't want to hurt anyone, especially you."

Maybe she'd have to reconsider her plans. Or maybe she needed to be careful about getting too close to Boone. She would have to continually remind herself that she was only a temporary caretaker, as she had been with the orphan babies.

"Come here, little one." She hefted him into her arms, and he came willingly, grabbing a fistful of her hair that had come loose after she'd taken off her hat. Without anyone telling her to fix it, she hadn't bothered with pulling it back up into a chignon.

She rather liked leaving it down and messy, something she hadn't been able to do in years. The waves of her hair nearly reached her waist and were soft and glossy, even after the past week without the maid's nightly ritual of brushing one hundred strokes.

She pressed a kiss against Boone's forehead and took a deep breath of his sweet baby scent—a mixture of baby powder and formula. "We shall get along just grand."

Boone babbled something nonsensical in response.

She laughed. "You agree, do you?"

When was the last time she'd laughed? She couldn't remember.

Boone's eyes widened again, almost as if laughter were a sound he wasn't familiar with either.

She laughed again.

A tentative smile worked its way up his lips.

It felt good to laugh for no reason other than she could. She twirled in a circle, and as she did so, Boone's smile widened.

"So, you like dancing?" She hummed a waltz and then started the steps she'd memorized long ago. As she did so, Boone continued to smile, and the sight of it was better than the mountain view outside the door.

At a sound from the door, she came to a sudden halt and spun to find Ryder filling the doorway. He stood motionless, his gaze riveted to her and Boone. He was disheveled and perspiring and breathing hard, as though he'd run the distance back to the ranch rather than riding his horse. His brows were furrowed, and his eyes were anxious.

Had he been worried about what he'd find upon his return?

She supposed it was only natural that he would be concerned about leaving his child with a stranger. "Boone's a good dancer already." She offered Ryder a smile now too.

Although his shoulders seemed to relax and his breathing evened out, his expression didn't contain anything even close to a smile. "Everything went okay, then?"

At the sound of Ryder's voice, Boone craned his head to see his father, his smile still bright and happy.

"Everything went perfectly." She held the baby out so that Ryder could see for himself that Boone was content and safe.

Ryder stepped inside and took the little fellow into his arms, brushing a kiss on top of the boy's head.

She liked that Ryder wasn't standoffish and showed affection to his son. Her own papa, though he'd been busy and important, had always made time for her and had never failed to shower her with affection.

"Did you find the reverend?" she asked as she made her way to the stove.

"He'll be here in a few minutes. I rode ahead."

She lifted the lid on the pot and let the aroma of the cooking vegetables fill her senses. It might not be a gourmet meal by one of the best chefs in the country, but she had the feeling it would be one of the best meals she'd ever tasted because she'd been able to make it.

She could feel Ryder watching her. "I hope you don't mind that I started supper."

"That's fine." His voice held a note of hesitation.

With a wooden spoon in hand, she glanced at him to find that his brows were still furrowed.

Had she overstepped herself by taking too much liberty? She didn't want to upset him, didn't want him to regret her being there. "I apologize. I should have asked you first before doing so."

"No, it's okay. You're free to do whatever you'd like."

She was *free*. A small unladylike part of her wanted to jump up and shout for joy at the sound of that word. But she reined in her enthusiasm and spoke calmly instead. "Thank you—"

"It's just that I don't want you to feel too burdened, like you have to do everything or anything." He situated Boone in his big arms, and the baby looked tiny in comparison.

"I do not feel burdened. I enjoyed making the soup."

"You did?"

Before she could reassure him again, a man slight of stature stepped into the doorway. From the clerical collar as well as prayer book he held, it was easy to see he was the reverend. Ryder introduced him as Reverend Livingston, and for several moments they made small talk about her journey, the beauty of Colorado, and the busyness of the harvesting season.

Ryder held Boone through the conversation with more proficiency than she'd ever witnessed from a man. Although Ryder wasn't talkative, he exuded a powerful presence nonetheless—one that wasn't domineering or intimidating but promised safety and security for those he cared about. In addition, she'd easily discerned that he was hardworking, tidy, and organized. She couldn't think of many men who could have managed all the responsibilities of both the ranch and a baby.

"Well, are you ready to begin?" the reverend asked.

Ryder shifted his attention from Boone to her. Only then did she realize she'd been staring at him again and that the reverend was watching her and had addressed the question to her.

Surely the reverend could understand she was simply trying to get to know Ryder a little bit more before pledging her life to him.

"I'm ready." She smoothed down her bodice and

skirt, the cotton material still unfamiliar to her touch compared to the silks and velvets and brocades she normally wore. She was as ready as she'd ever be for the strange circumstances in which she found herself. Never when she was a girl and imagining her wedding day would she have pictured herself marrying a stranger in a rustic cabin in the high country of Colorado.

When she questioned the need for witnesses, the reverend explained that in Colorado, the marriage was legal without witnesses—that in fact, his own presence wasn't entirely necessary either but would help solemnize the occasion.

The reverend opened the prayer book and read a prayer, then several Scriptures. She had a difficult time concentrating on the words and instead was thinking about her papa and what he would say if he could see her now. Would he be disappointed that she'd run away? Or would he understand she'd felt she had no other choice?

He'd always wanted the best for her, had always given her everything, had never denied her anything. He'd risked spoiling her as his only child. And he very well could have except that he'd loved her so immensely and thoroughly that she couldn't keep from adoring him in return and wanting to please him.

When he'd met Lenora, a widowed New York socialite from an upstanding family, Genevieve hadn't necessarily liked the idea of letting someone else into their family. After all, she and Papa had gotten along just fine for fifteen years, and they hadn't needed anyone else.

But of course, she'd loved her papa so dearly that she'd wanted him to get married if that would make him happy. At the time, she'd believed he was starting to prepare for the day when his only daughter would get married and he would be alone. But in hindsight, she realized he'd known he was sick with cancer, and he'd been preparing for her future instead. He'd thought that by marrying Lenora, he would be leaving her with a mother who could guide her and help her through the years until she had a husband.

He'd died only a year after the wedding to Lenora. For months, even the first couple of years after his passing, Genevieve hadn't been able to function amidst her consuming grief, and she'd felt as though she were living in a bad dream.

She could give her stepmother credit for keeping her from sinking too far into her melancholy. Lenora had stepped in and taken charge of everything—visitors, finances, the servants, the social calendar, the houses, the business managers, and even speaking with the lawyers.

Genevieve had been grateful to give all control to Lenora—at least, at first. But as time had elapsed, her grief had diminished, and she'd eventually been ready to regain her life.

She'd tried to prove she was strong, but the damage

had already been done. Lenora saw her as a weak and frail woman and couldn't be persuaded to change her view. It didn't matter that Genevieve had finally been able to accept her papa's death. It didn't matter that she'd grown up and matured. It didn't matter that she was ready to shoulder more responsibility. As Genevieve tried to pull away, Lenora only tightened her hold.

Of course, Lenora was trying to be a good stepmother and guardian. Genevieve had tried to understand that. With the stipulations of Papa's will, Lenora was required to take care of Genevieve if she wanted to claim her portion of the inheritance on Genevieve's twenty-first birthday. But the trouble was that Lenora was taking her duties much too seriously.

Hopefully, if her papa were watching from heaven, he'd understand that Lenora's grip had been strangling the life from Genevieve and that running away had been her only option.

"Wilt thou have this woman to be thy wedded wife, to live together after God's ordinance in the holy estate of Matrimony? Wilt thou love her, comfort her, honor, and keep her, in sickness and in health? And forsaking all others, keep thee only to her, so long as you both shall live?"

"I will." Ryder didn't hesitate. His declaration was firm and filled with determination.

The reverend shifted to her and began the same

question: "Wilt thou have this man to be thy wedded husband, to live together after God's ordinance in the holy estate of Matrimony? Wilt thou obey him and serve him, love, honor, and keep him, in sickness and in health? And forsaking all others, keep thee only to him, so long as you both shall live?"

She swallowed the swift protest that seemed to rise out of nowhere. How could she make this kind of vow, one that promised to love him as long as she lived? She couldn't. Not when she was planning to leave him in a year.

She blew out a stiff breath. What was she doing? She'd already lied once about her name. And if she took the vow, she'd be lying again.

"Constance?" the reverend prompted, clearly having heard about Constance Franklin enough over recent weeks that the switch in names was now an adjustment. "I mean, Genevieve?"

She quickly nodded. What choice did she have now that she was here? Everything was already set in motion, and she couldn't back out now. "I will."

She would do her best to honor her vow over the next year and do everything in it to the best of her ability . . . for at least a year. Surely that was good enough.

The rest of the ceremony was a blur, even the part where Ryder gave her a ring—a plain gold band without any embellishments or jewels or engravings. It was likely the simplest piece of jewelry she'd ever worn, especially compared to the rings and bracelets and necklaces she had in her chatelaine. She'd sold off another small piece in Denver to ensure she had enough to survive for a while, but she still had at least a dozen other items left.

As the reverend closed in prayer, asking God to bless the union, she held out her hand just enough to see the ring on her finger. It might be simple, but it was symbolic of her freedom. And she couldn't forget that.

Once the wedding was finished, they signed a marriage certificate. Genevieve hadn't been sure which name to sign, Constance's or hers, so in the end, she'd simply written Genevieve and left off her family name. Thankfully, the reverend hadn't said anything about it or perhaps had been too busy chatting to notice.

She invited him to stay for a bowl of soup and found canned peaches to serve with it. Although the meal was meatless, no one complained. In fact, Ryder refilled his bowl two times.

After the reverend started on his way back to Breckenridge, Ryder left the cabin to do the *evening chores*, as he called them. She offered to assist, but he assured her that she was helping enough by watching Boone.

She busied herself cleaning up the meal. By then Boone was fussing again with hungry grunts. She hurried to prepare him a bottle and then settled into the rocking chair beside the stove.

At the silence and the warmth and the security, she felt for the first time in days as though she could finally cease looking over her shoulder and worrying that someone would see her and catch her.

She closed her eyes and relaxed, but the moment she did so, the exhaustion of the past week caught up with her and slumber claimed her.

7

Ryder paused outside the cabin door and listened. The trill of katydids echoed in the darkness of the summer night, but the inside of the cabin was quiet. Too quiet.

His pulse picked up pace as it had when he'd been riding home from Breckenridge, his mind unable to stop replaying the day Sadie had left him. He'd come home from a rough day with his cattle after having to put down one of the heifers that had been attacked by a wolf and mangled too badly to survive. When he'd walked into his new home that wintery February day, he'd shaken the snow from his coat and unwound the scarf covering his face and head, ready to tell Sadie all about the tragic tale—one full of adventure and danger, just the way she liked.

But she hadn't been inside the cabin. She hadn't been in the privy or the smokehouse or the barn. He'd searched and called out for her until he'd been almost frantic, half believing the horse thieves who'd had a role in killing Pa Oakley were back in the area and had kidnapped her.

He'd finally gone back into the cabin intending to don his warmest clothing and ride down to High C Ranch and ask his brother to form a search party for Sadie. He'd been gathering more ammunition for his revolver when he'd realized her bag was gone.

He hadn't needed to look around much longer to discover that not only was her bag gone but also every single thing she'd owned or brought to the cabin—which hadn't been much. In that moment, his gut had twisted with the truth.

She hadn't been taken. She'd left him.

He'd ridden straightaway to her family home, a ramshackle place on the southern edge of Breckenridge. Captain Moore, her father, had answered Ryder's banging with shouts and curses, as drunk as always.

Once a renowned captain in the War of the Rebellion, Sadie's father coped with the tragedies that haunted him the only way he knew: by drinking himself into oblivion every day. That meant his wife and three daughters, including Sadie, were largely unsupervised and did whatever they pleased most of the time.

The captain hadn't known where Sadie was. After Ryder's shouting and threats, one of Sadie's sisters had finally come to the door and admitted that Sadie had gone straight to Axe Lyman. Apparently, she'd started seeing Axe after Ryder had stopped coming around, even once she'd learned she was carrying Ryder's baby. And apparently the only reason she'd agreed to get married was because Ryder had convinced her that he'd provide a good life.

But the life he'd given her that first week of marriage had been anything but good. It had been lonely and isolated and barren. She'd learned Ryder didn't have any wealth and wouldn't be able to buy her all the things she'd hoped he would. She'd learned he was boring and simple. She'd learned her future would be dull and filled with the work of growing a ranch and taking care of a baby.

And so she'd gone back to Axe.

Ryder gripped the door handle. What if the same thing happened with Genevieve? She'd learn soon enough, as Sadie had, that he was poor and boring and simple, that her future would be dull and filled with work and caring for a baby. What if, after a week or a month or even a year, she gave up and decided to leave him?

He knew he couldn't compare the two women. It wasn't fair to Genevieve when she'd been nothing but honest and kind from the moment she'd first sent him a letter. Yes, she'd described her eye color differently in her letter. On his way to get the reverend, he'd re-read the letter that he kept in his coat pocket. He'd wanted to be sure he hadn't imagined that she'd claimed to have brown eyes. He wasn't sure why she'd said so when her eyes were a pale blue. Maybe she was embarrassed to have such a unique eye color. Maybe she hadn't been sure how to describe the color to him. Maybe she'd assumed he wouldn't like her if she mentioned the blue-gray color.

Whatever the case, it was a tiny thing. Probably not even worth bringing up. Especially since he'd sensed a sweetness and kindness in her since the moment she'd first dismounted from her horse.

And seeing her dancing with Boone when he'd returned from fetching the reverend? He'd never witnessed anything more beautiful. Her long dark hair had been unbound and swirling around her, practically begging him to touch the strands and test for himself whether they were as thick and silky as they looked.

He imagined she resembled one of the Greek goddesses he'd read about in the ancient myths— confident, strong, and too beautiful for this world. He pictured her in a flowing white gown, with layers of material floating around her, complementing her pale skin and making her dark hair all the more startling and her lips all the redder.

"Come on," he whispered to himself with a sharp mental shake. This was exactly the sort of fantasizing he couldn't allow himself. After the mistakes he'd made with other women, including Sadie, he didn't want to allow his manly urges to dictate his life again. He needed to remain in control and have better self-discipline.

Besides, after the pain he'd experienced from his failed marriage, he didn't want to jump into another relationship so soon. He'd made that clear enough in the letter he'd written to Constance—to Genevieve—the one she carried with her the same way he carried hers. He'd told her he wouldn't place the usual wifely expectations and demands upon her, that he just wanted her to be a mother to Boone.

And that was still true. He didn't want to get involved physically with another woman, especially not a woman he didn't know and love. He'd had enough casual affairs in his life already. And the next time he had relations with a woman, he wanted to do it right, out of love and not selfish need.

Maybe someday he'd develop love for Genevieve. And maybe she would for him too. If that happened and they wanted to have more, they could decide on that together. But until then, he had to learn to be satisfied with a marriage of convenience . . . in spite of how attractive his new wife was.

He opened the door a crack and listened again. It was still too quiet.

He didn't want to assume the worst had happened, but as he swung the door wider, his gaze anxiously shot around the room until he caught sight of her in the rocker beside the stove, asleep with Boone in her arms.

The rapid beat of his heart slowed. She was still here, and he'd worried for nothing.

After barring the door as quietly as possible, he crossed to the rocker and stood in front of her, unsure what to do. As if sensing his presence, Boone opened his eyes and peered up at him. He was tucked securely into Genevieve's arms, and there was no chance of him slipping out.

Even so, Ryder gently lifted the child away from her. As he did so, she stirred, opened her eyes, and smiled sleepily up at him. "Thank you. I certainly am more tired than I realized."

"It's all right." He gathered Boone close. "I'll get Boone ready for bed since you had a long day."

Her dark lashes had already fallen, fanning out over her pale skin. When she didn't respond or move except for the rhythmic rise and fall of her chest, he guessed she'd fallen back asleep.

He changed Boone's diaper, placed him in his nightclothes, and wrapped him up tightly in one of his blankets. Within no time, the baby fell back asleep too.

After settling him in his cradle, Ryder straightened and took in Genevieve, still resting in the rocker.

What exactly would he do for the sleeping arrangements for the night? Since he'd already told her they wouldn't consummate their marriage, they couldn't use the same bed, could they?

But what other choice did they have?

He glanced around the cabin again, then jammed his fingers into his hair as if that could somehow keep him from worrying. It never did.

There had never been any talk about abstaining between him and Sadie. He'd never once considered it, and neither had she, and they'd shared the bed the way any married couple would.

But this time, things were different.

He took in the space available in the rest of the cabin. There wasn't much room. But if he pushed the table and chairs aside, he could make a spot big enough for a bedroll on the floor.

He dug his fingers deeper into his hair. He didn't want to go to all that trouble every night. Besides, how long would such a sleeping arrangement last? He could do it for a short while. But what if it turned into endless weeks? It would get awfully cold once the night temperatures started dropping in a month or so with the coming of autumn.

Blowing out an exasperated breath, he turned his attention to the bed. It was big enough to sleep two people. They could each have their sides and wouldn't have to touch. After all, they were legally married, and there was nothing sinful about lying next to his wife in bed.

Yes, that's what they'd do. They'd share the bed right

from the start. Wasn't any reason why they shouldn't . . . except maybe a little awkwardness, since they didn't know each other yet. But they'd eventually grow more comfortable, and it wouldn't seem so strange. Might as well not put off the inevitable.

His gaze bounced back to her in the rocker. She was still sleeping, her head tilted, her face peaceful.

Even if she looked peaceful enough, he needed to wake her up so that she could get into bed.

He crossed to her again and stood over her, giving himself permission to stare at her since she was asleep and wouldn't have to know how smitten he was with her— her elegant features, the pretty set of her mouth, her perfectly rounded chin, and her graceful neck. Her dark hair was still unbound and framed her face, falling in gentle waves all around her.

Why was she here with him when she could have any man she wanted? The question echoed through him, this time louder than earlier.

As she sighed a tired breath and shifted as though to get more comfortable, his chest swelled with an unexplainable emotion. Was it compassion for her? She was obviously exhausted from her journey.

Maybe he shouldn't wake her and should instead just place her in bed. Without giving himself the chance to overthink the situation any longer, he bent and slipped his arms under her. After years of working the land and taking care of horses and cattle, he had no trouble lifting her.

As he situated her against his chest, her lashes rose again, and her blue-gray eyes met his and filled with confusion.

"You fell asleep in the chair," he whispered as he started across the room. "So I'm putting you in bed. That's all."

"Oh dear." Her tone held chagrin. "I apologize for the trouble."

"No trouble."

"You may put me down, and I'll manage."

"You're fine." He reached the edge of the bed and lowered her carefully. "Go on back to sleep."

"I cannot . . ." Her eyelids closed, and her voice trailed off. She didn't move, didn't protest. She'd fallen asleep again.

He scanned the length of her. Her skirt and bodice were slightly too big for her. Even though they were dusty from the traveling, the material was crisp and unstained, as if it were new. Her leather boots were of excellent quality, well-polished and sturdy—not at all what he would have expected of a poor orphanage worker.

Should he take off her shoes for the night?

He bent and touched one of the laces, the hem of her skirt falling high enough that he could also see one of her stockings, which was made of fine knit silk, a quality he'd never seen before.

She had slender legs, and the stockings rose high above her calf, likely to her knees. He had the urge to run his finger along the soft material—only to feel it, not her. But he pulled his hand away and straightened.

No, he'd maintain better self-control if he didn't think about undressing her in any way—not even to take off her shoes and stockings. In fact, it would be for the best to keep his hands off her at all times.

He retrieved an extra blanket from under the bed and draped it over her. He tidied up the house, banked the embers in the stove, checked on Boone one last time, then snuffed the lantern before shedding his clothing down to his underdrawers.

As he stepped up to the bed on the opposite side of Genevieve, he hesitated. Even though he always slept in his underdrawers and nothing else, maybe he needed to at least keep on a shirt. He bent, picked up his undershirt, and began to tug it back over his head. But at the waft of perspiration lingering in the material from the heat of the summer day, he tossed the item back to the ground.

Whether or not he was decent, he was going shirtless. That's all there was to it.

He lowered himself to the edge of the bed, the mattress creaking under his weight. He held himself stiffly, waiting for her to awaken and protest his presence. But only stillness and silence came from her side of the bed.

Carefully, he spread out on top, not wanting to make too much commotion by trying to pull the covers down. Thankfully, the night was still warm and balmy, and he had no need for a blanket at the moment. If he got cold during the night, he'd cover up then.

As he lay straight as a poker stick and stared up at the dark log ceiling beams, the only thought in his mind was that there was a beautiful woman in bed beside him—a beautiful woman who also happened to be his wife. What was he doing lying there? He was only asking for trouble. Obviously not tonight or anytime real soon. He wasn't a brute who would ever force himself on any woman.

But he also wasn't a saint. His son was proof of that. If at some point in the future he reached for her and she didn't resist his overtures, there was no telling what could happen.

That meant he couldn't ever reach for her in bed— especially while they were in bed.

With a soft growl of frustration at himself for his weakness, he rolled so that he was facing away from her. He had to pretend she wasn't there. And even though pretending he was alone wouldn't solve all his problems, hopefully he'd be able to prove to himself and to her that he was a man of honor.

8

Genevieve didn't want to wake up. She was so comfortable and her sleep so sound that she couldn't remember the last time she'd slept so well.

But at the slight brush of fingers against her hair, wakefulness prodded her, and she opened her eyes. The hint of dawn greeted her with enough light to take in her surroundings. Log walls, log beams, a one-room cabin.

Memories of the previous day rushed back to her all at once. She'd arrived on the stagecoach in Frisco, she'd ridden out to the ranch, and she'd gotten married to Ryder Oakley. It had been a very full day, and she must have fallen asleep at some point, because she couldn't remember how she'd ended up in the bed.

But clearly that's where she was.

Where was Ryder? And Boone?

With a strange panic pulsing through her, she started to sit up only to find an arm draped across her. From the muscular size, she knew it could only belong to one person: Ryder. And his arm was bare, which meant he wasn't wearing clothing—or at least, wasn't wearing a shirt.

Heat swept into her face, and she reclined against the mattress, holding herself rigid.

She waited for him to say something or to roll away, but he remained relaxed, as if he were accustomed to lying beside a woman and holding her in bed.

Maybe he was. Obviously he'd done so before. But what about his letter and his sentence: *I promise you'll have complete freedom from the usual demands.* Had he changed his mind already? Would he expect more from the marriage bed after all? Did he want a real wife and not just a mother to his baby?

As his fingers grazed her ribs, she closed her eyes and swallowed hard against the need to push him away and scramble out of the bed.

What had happened last night? Had she been so tired that she'd fallen into his arms and into his bed? Had they ended up doing something after all? If so, surely she would have remembered it.

She mentally scanned herself. She was still wearing her clothing, even her stockings and shoes. And a blanket was tucked securely around her.

His hand upon her ribs moved again, tugging gently through her hair.

Were his fingers entwined in her hair?

Embarrassment shifted through her again. It was certainly forward of him to be touching her so boldly after only knowing her for such a short time. Should she scoot away from him and remind him of what he'd told her in the letter?

She closed her eyes and tried to think.

This was an awkward situation. Or was it? She was married to him. And this was what married people did. After all, he only had one bed, and it was natural they should share it. What had she expected? That they'd have separate sleeping quarters for the next year?

She certainly hadn't imagined they'd end up beside each other in bed, with him half holding her.

He stretched, his arm tightening over her. In the next second, he jerked back, removing his arm from her and rolling over, putting at least a foot of distance between them.

Did his waking reaction mean he hadn't meant to touch her? That the closeness had been accidental?

She breathed a sigh. At the same time, she heard him expel a tight breath.

"Good morning," she whispered. She may as well let him know she was awake.

He released a frustrated groan. "I'm sorry about that. Was hoping you were still asleep and wouldn't realize I'd accidentally touched you."

Her body relaxed against the mattress even more. He wasn't breaking his word after all. "It's all right. We are in rather close quarters."

As he folded his bare arms behind his head, his bare chest stretched out next to her. Although the room was still dark with the lingering shadows of the night, she could see enough to know that his chest was smooth and solid and hard.

Not that she was giving herself permission to look. But she could admit she was fascinated by him— fascinated that a half-naked man was in the bed beside her, fascinated by the male physique, fascinated by the privilege of marriage that allowed for such intimacy.

As fascinating as everything was, it was also entirely scandalous for a lady like her to be thinking so brazenly about a man. A part of her demanded that she climb out of the bed at once and set a precedent for the days to come, that she wouldn't tolerate such familiarity. But if she'd wanted to avoid scandal, she wouldn't have left home to begin with.

The truth was, she would need to make the best of the situation, and doing so meant she couldn't act like a prude every time he was unclothed or they shared the bed. Because apparently they were going to sleep together while at the same time abstaining from . . . intimacies.

She could certainly do so. Although she liked Ryder so far, she wasn't interested in him beyond the partnership he'd mentioned. He would allow her to live on his ranch, and she would take care of the home and his son. That was all she needed.

At the same time, she didn't have to jump out of bed and scramble to get away from him. She could make an effort to get to know him better, couldn't she?

"I really like your ranch," she said softly.

"You do?" His response was just as soft and tinged with surprise.

"It's very lovely."

He was silent for several beats. "I'm glad you like it."

Did his voice hold relief? Had he been worried about how she'd like living there? Was it possible his previous wife hadn't been appreciative of the home he'd tried to make for her?

"You picked a wonderful place for the cabin," she added. "The view from the front door is stunning."

"I planned it that way."

"I suspected so." She situated her head on her pillow, starting to feel more comfortable beside him. "Did you always want to be a rancher?"

He shrugged. "After growing up ranching, reckon it's what I know."

"Will you tell me about your family?" she asked tentatively, not wanting to probe. "The livery owner, Virgil, told me some yesterday, but I would like to hear more."

For a short while, they talked about his family's ranch, High Country Ranch five miles to the south. He told her briefly about how he and his brother had been adopted by the Oakleys, who had two sons and twin daughters. His two adoptive brothers had recently gotten married, and one of the twins had also gotten married and moved out of the country to be with her husband. The other twin sister had helped him take care of Boone over the summer, but she had a thriving candy-making business in Breckenridge and was busy with that.

"I've always wondered what it would be like to have a large family," Genevieve said wistfully, now on her side, facing him.

"You don't have any siblings?" He was on his side too, resting his head on his arm. The light was growing, and the outline of his face was more visible—strong features, an intense gaze, and a serious set to his mouth.

"No, I was an only child. It was just my papa and me."

"Were you close to him?" Ryder's question was hesitant, as though he suspected this was a sensitive topic.

"Very." Her throat closed up with emotion, and she could say no more. Even though she had worked through her grief, talking about her papa still wasn't easy.

Ryder reached out and squeezed her arm as though to reassure her that she didn't need to say any more, that he understood how much she'd loved her papa.

She laid a hand on top of his and squeezed back to thank him for his kind gesture. And for a long moment they lay that way, their hands touching, the grief palpable.

At a gruntlike cry from the cradle at the end of the bed, she shoved herself up and kicked off the blanket that Ryder must have tucked around her. Even as she scrambled toward Boone, Ryder remained where he was, clearly not feeling the same urgency.

She gathered the baby in her arms, expecting him to be startled to see her, to want Ryder instead and perhaps to fuss. But he watched her as he had yesterday, with wide eyes as though he'd hoped to see her again. Or was that just wishful thinking on her part?

"He likes you." Ryder had pushed up and was leaning back on his elbows, his legs casually crossed, watching her through heavy-lidded eyes.

"I hope so." From her position at the end of the bed, and with even more light spilling past the curtains, she had full view of him, unclad except for his underdrawers. His body was more magnificent than she'd imagined, all sinewy muscles and taut flesh and hard planes.

With a flush quickly forming in her cheeks, she buried her face against Boone's downy head. Even though she'd had suitors over the past couple of years, including Prescott, Lenora had regulated every visit. Genevieve had never even held hands with a man, never come close to kissing one, and certainly had never seen a man without his clothing on.

As though realizing her discomfort at his state of undress, Ryder finally sat up and swung his legs over the edge of the bed. He swiped up a pair of trousers from the floor and stuffed his legs inside.

When he stood and began to pull them up, she couldn't make herself look away, even though she was being much too brazen in watching a man get attired. As he reached for a dangling suspender, he paused and cast a glance her way.

Rapidly, she spun away from him, tempted to fan her face.

What was wrong with her? Why was she behaving like a loose woman? Was it because she wasn't under anyone's supervision now? Because every action had been regulated for so long she didn't know how to control herself?

Pursing her lips with fresh determination to behave, she crossed to the stove, grabbed a handful of kindling from the wood box, then added it to the low glow of embers. A moment later, flames sprang to life. Just like that.

Was that how it was with lust too? Just a little kindling could fuel a fire?

At the soft sliding of more clothing, she forced herself not to turn and look at Ryder again. As nice as he was and as pleasant as their whispered conversation in bed had been moments ago, she had no interest in anything more developing between them.

Of course, she wanted to have a cordial relationship with him, and she hoped they would work well together. She wouldn't mind getting to know him better and even developing a friendship.

But all other thoughts, including those about his body and him getting dressed, needed to be forever banished and never allowed to roam free.

9

He'd been married for five days, and Genevieve hadn't left him yet.

From his mount, Ryder glanced sideways at her on her horse beside him, needing to reassure himself that she was still with him.

"Do you think your family will like me?" she asked as they passed under the smooth log of the gate emblazoned with black metal letters that read: *High Country Ranch.*

On either side of the entrance, split-rail fencing ran the length of the wide-open grassland where the horses and cattle grazed. Ahead, a dirt road wound back for a quarter of a mile through a woodland of pines and led to the main house, situated at the base of a slope. Pa Oakley had designed the layout of the ranch well, because the buffer of trees helped to protect the barns and livestock from the wind and snow and drifts that were prevalent over the long winter months.

He could feel Genevieve's eyes upon him, waiting for an answer to his question.

"They'll like you just fine." Boone began to stir after napping the whole ride to the ranch, and Ryder gave him a gentle pat in the sling on his chest. Genevieve had offered to carry Boone, but Ryder had gotten used to traveling with the baby in the sling and figured it would free up Genevieve for the ride. Besides, he hadn't worn the sling since Genevieve had arrived, and he could admit he missed the closeness it provided with Boone.

"I do hope they will approve of me." Her gaze was sweeping over the herd of horses in the south pasture, the dozens of varieties Pa Oakley had bred and that Maverick was now overseeing. Even if Maverick had experienced a rocky start to taking over the ranch, Ryder was proud of his brother for how he'd persevered. Maverick had also finally married his best friend's sister after years of denying his feelings for her.

Ryder didn't expect the kind of love Maverick shared with his wife, but he anticipated that his family would like Genevieve more than *just fine,* much better than they'd ever liked Sadie. But he couldn't say that and refused to talk bad about Sadie to his new wife, even though he didn't have much good to say about Boone's mother.

"Will you tell me about the different breeds your family has?" she asked, her gaze still riveted to the horses.

The herds did make a pretty picture, grazing on the open range with the mountains rising majestically behind them.

So did Genevieve. Her dark hair was pulled up and pinned beneath a straw hat, giving him a view of her slender neck, a delicate stretch of her throat, and her collarbones. The green calico bodice and skirt she'd donned that morning appeared to be another new garment—one he doubted she'd ever worn before.

He wasn't sure how she'd afforded to buy so many clothes. Maybe he should have warned her his ranch wasn't anything fancy and she'd be fine in her old garments. Or perhaps she was used to wearing fine clothing—if her stockings and shoes were any indication. The trouble was, what happened when she wanted to buy more and he couldn't purchase what she was accustomed to having?

He shook away the thought and instead focused on talking to her about the horses. He liked when she asked him questions about the ranch and livestock. It showed she was interested, and that's what he wanted. He wanted her to like ranch life and the West, even though it was a difficult way of living at times.

So far over the past five days since her arrival, she'd seemed to adjust well enough, and they'd fallen into an easy routine. During the days, he worked with his cattle and managed the herd and other livestock while she stayed close to the cabin and tended Boone. She'd cooked a few meals, but from the simplicity of the fare, he guessed she didn't have many recipes or was inexperienced. Either way, she'd tried, and he appreciated her efforts.

She'd admitted to not knowing about vegetable gardens and had asked him astute questions about how to weed, trim back, and harvest the ripe produce. She'd also asked him about the chickens and how to gather eggs, blaming her ignorance on having lived in the city.

In the evenings, when he stepped out to check on the livestock and close up the barn, she had the privacy of the cabin to change into a nightgown and complete her nightly ritual. By the time he returned, Boone was laid down and she already asleep in bed.

Ryder had continued to share the bed with her and had done well keeping his hands to himself each night. Every now and then, his arm ended up around her, as it had that first morning he'd awoken to find himself touching her. He'd tried to be more careful, but his body was attuned to her presence near him, regardless of how hard he was working to maintain self-control. And how hard he was working to sleep lightly so that he didn't have any nightmares.

He especially liked the early morning hour at daybreak, when they were both awake. She was never in a rush to get out of bed and lay beside him while they whispered about life. Most of the time, they talked about Boone or the tasks of the day ahead. But sometimes he shared more about his family, and she'd talked fondly about her papa. He'd finally been able to ask her about Open Door Asylum, which she'd mentioned in her letter, and she'd spoken of all she'd done there and how much it had meant to her to be a part of the orphanage.

He'd already gotten to know her better than he had any other woman. The truth was, the more time he spent with her, the more he liked her. And he was coming to realize just how lucky he'd been—or perhaps Providence had a hand in things—to have Genevieve respond to his letter and come west to be a part of his and Boone's lives.

As they entered the woodland and lost sight of the herd, his heart gave a small kick of something he hadn't felt in a long time. Hope. Could he have hope for his future? For a family of his own? He hadn't believed it possible, especially after losing Sadie.

But with Genevieve, what if he could allow himself to hope for everything he'd never thought he'd have?

Genevieve had moved ahead of him, enough that he could see her profile. With the way she was sitting in the saddle, her usually baggy clothing hugged her form, giving a rare view of her womanly curves.

"Have you considered raising horses?" She tossed the question over her shoulder, catching him staring at her.

She simply held his gaze, the blue-gray as stunning as

always. It was holding him captive more and more often, so that he didn't want to look away.

One of her delicate brows arched, reminding him that she was waiting for his answer. He shrugged. "I don't love horses the way Maverick does."

She shifted her focus back to the wagon path ahead of them. "What do you love, Ryder?"

The question took him so much by surprise that he almost yanked on the reins and brought his mount to a halt. What did he love? No one had ever asked him that question before.

His mind raced to find an answer. Had he really ever loved anything? Sure, he liked ranching, liked the beauty of the West, liked the satisfaction that came after a day of hard work. But did he love it?

He couldn't claim the same passion for ranching the other ranchers in Summit County did. But it was all he really knew and would give him a good life if he was able to build his herd.

Even so, the only thing that really mattered to him was Boone. And the rest of his brothers and sisters. "Reckon I love my family more than anything else."

"That is easy to see." She smiled over her shoulder at him, and the beautiful curve of her lips sent his stomach tumbling end over end. "But what else? What do you enjoy most?"

Right now he was enjoying the ride with her and

getting his fair share of looking at her. But he couldn't say that. He had to think of something that didn't make him sound like a bumbling idiot.

"You know I like history . . ."

One night during supper, she'd asked him about his book collection. They'd ended up talking about their favorite novels, and he'd learned that she was well-educated and well-read for an orphan. He'd shared with her about his love of studying history, and she'd told him that her papa had a collection of history books.

"And . . ." she prompted.

He pushed past his reticence and blurted out, "Over the past couple of years, I've started investigating and writing down the history of Colorado."

She abruptly reined in her horse and shifted around so that she was facing him directly.

With her curious eyes studying his face, he ducked his head beneath the brim of his Stetson. Why had he brought up his project? He rarely discussed it with anyone, except for the old-timers like Virgil in Frisco, who'd been in Colorado since the beginning. "I mostly do the chronicling during the winter months when I'm not so busy. I've collected firsthand tales from some people who were here even before the gold rush."

"That's incredible." Her eyes began to shine with admiration.

"Really?" So she didn't find the hobby odd?

"I love it that you're doing something so worthwhile."

He'd never been entirely sure what he liked about studying history. Maybe it made him feel connected with the past, something that had been torn from him brutally the day his real parents had been slaughtered. Maybe in finding the history of others, he could preserve for others what he couldn't preserve for himself.

Whatever the case, Pa Oakley had been the one to encourage him to write down Colorado's history so that it wouldn't be forgotten. Now he had almost an entire book of stories.

At a call from down the wagon path near the clearing, he dragged his attention away from Genevieve to find that Clementine was waving at them. Her blond-red hair hung in a long braid over her shoulder, and she was barefoot, making her look younger than her nineteen years.

"You can't keep her all to yourself, Ryder," his sister yelled with a wide grin.

He could admit he was tempted to keep Genevieve to himself. He'd only agreed to bring her to supper because Maverick had pestered him into it the other day when he'd ridden over to the ranch without her. Of course, Maverick had already heard about the arrival of the bride and the hasty evening wedding. Seemed as though the news had spread quicker than wildfire all across the county.

Whatever the case, Ryder had to introduce Genevieve

to everyone sooner or later. And tonight was as good a night as any.

They made their way to the ranch yard, an open patch of grass that filled the area between the house and the barns. The log cabin was the original home Pa Oakley had built fourteen years ago when they'd arrived in Summit County and claimed their homestead. Over the years, they'd added several rooms to the structure, but the rustic look of the home remained the same. It was a place that would always be special to him because it had been the first real home he'd had since he was five.

Clementine greeted Genevieve warmly with a hug. And a moment later, Maverick and Hazel stumbled out of the mare barn flushed, disheveled, and brushing straw from their clothing. As always, the sight of the two of them so in love made Ryder's chest clench with an emotion he couldn't name but that bordered on jealousy. They welcomed Genevieve as enthusiastically as Clementine.

"Supper's ready," Clementine said as she led the way toward the raised front porch of the cabin, cuddling Boone as she did so.

The cabin door ahead opened, and a man stepped out hesitantly. It was Tanner. Although slightly taller than Ryder, they shared similar broad facial features and broad shoulders. While they had the same brown hair and eyes, Tanner always needed a haircut, and his eyes were always full of humor.

Even now, Tanner offered one of his charming grins.

Ryder halted abruptly and glared at him. "What's he doing here?"

Beside him, Genevieve had also come to a halt, and she was taking in Tanner, likely seeing the striking family resemblance.

Clementine turned her green eyes full of censure upon Ryder. "Now, come on, Ryder. Tanner heard you got married and came to meet your new wife."

Ryder bit back a caustic comment. For as much conflict as he and Tanner had experienced over recent months, Tanner was still his flesh and blood, and Ryder would do anything for him. He'd spent years of his life sacrificing for his little brother, protecting him, keeping him happy, and making sure they stayed together.

But apparently that wasn't enough for Tanner. *Ryder* wasn't enough. Because ever since Pa Oakley had died in January, Tanner had been on a mission to find more information about their past—who their parents were, and where they'd come from. He'd even hired an investigator.

It was almost as if Pa Oakley's death had given Tanner the freedom he'd been waiting for to explore their roots. Perhaps Tanner hadn't wanted to offend their adoptive pa with that kind of search. Perhaps he hadn't wanted to seem ungrateful for all that Pa Oakley had done for them.

Whatever the case, Ryder had opposed Tanner stirring up the past, had told him to let it go. But of course, Tanner was as stubborn as an old mule. And he'd persisted with his quest in spite of Ryder's objections.

They'd had some terrible arguments about it. The last one had been especially difficult because Tanner had grown accusatory, complaining that Ryder knew more than he was willing to share. They'd ended up yelling at each other in a wrestling match because Tanner hadn't been able to accept that Ryder didn't have any names or places or details to give him.

"How much information do you think a five-year-old can remember?" Ryder had shouted at his brother. "It was twenty years ago. I don't have any memories, so stop hounding me."

"Maybe you just have to make yourself remember," Tanner had shouted back, his features taut with a desperation Ryder hadn't liked. Tanner had been three at the time they'd lost their family and had no memories of that fateful day either.

"Some things are best forgotten." Ryder's voice had been hard and his statement final the last time he'd spoken with Tanner. And now, today, here his brother was.

If only Tanner would let the past stay where it belonged.

"It's good to see you too, Ryder." Tanner was still

smiling, as carefree and happy as always.

Ryder's chest swelled. That's all he'd ever wanted for his brother—for him to be carefree and happy. So why did he have the feeling he'd failed?

10

Genevieve liked Ryder's family immensely.

As they finished the evening meal and Clementine passed around a platter with samples of her candy, Genevieve allowed herself a moment of satisfaction. She took in the face of each person around the table, the large and noisy Oakley clan, the love evident in all the conversations and teasing.

The tension between Ryder and his brother Tanner was present as well, although she'd sensed Ryder trying hard to remain polite throughout the meal.

Regardless, she'd never enjoyed a meal more than she had with the Oakleys. Their teasing and laughter and sharing had been everything she'd imagined it would be like in a big family. Of course, she and Papa had always teased and laughed and shared too. They'd had many adventures, especially traveling the world and seeing countless cultures and places. She wouldn't have traded her precious time with him for any reason.

But a part of her had secretly wished for a bigger family—one like the Oakleys, who supported and encouraged and loved each other through all the joys and sorrows of life. Even extended family would have been a blessing, but except for a few distant relatives on her mother's side of the family, she'd had no one but Papa growing up.

Across the long table in the cozy kitchen, Tanner finished relaying another story about his adventures in the mountains and then settled his gaze upon Genevieve with unabashed interest. "I heard you were a fine lady, and now I can see that's true."

In the middle of tasting a delectable chocolate with mixed fruit and nuts, Genevieve froze. A lady? Was that what people were saying about her? And if so, why? Hadn't she made herself inconspicuous with her quaint clothing and simple lifestyle?

If word about her being a fine lady was spreading, how long would it take before someone connected her with the missing heiress?

From the chair beside her, Ryder shifted and pinned Tanner with a hard look.

Genevieve wasn't sure what was causing the discord between the two men, but Ryder and Tanner hadn't spoken more than a few words to each other during the entire meal.

It was easy to distinguish the familial relationship. Both were handsome men, with their warm brown eyes and angular, almost distinguished features. But the two were entirely opposite in personality. Tanner was more sociable and loquacious. Ryder, on the other hand, was introspective and quiet.

"So, Genevieve. Tell us more about yourself." The way Tanner said her name sounded almost as though he was questioning whether it really belonged to her.

Was he? Or was she projecting her insecurities and fears about being discovered? Over dinner she'd learned he traveled a great deal as a fur trapper and trail guide in the Rockies. Perhaps during a recent expedition, he'd spotted the news about her and had already questioned if she was the same Genevieve mentioned in the article.

"We'd love to hear more about your past." Tanner reclined casually.

Or was there something in his posture that was tense, as though he was hinting that he wanted her to tell the whole truth instead of hiding behind Constance Franklin's identity?

She hesitated. "I don't know where to start."

"You don't have to start anywhere." Ryder was speaking to her, but his gaze was upon Tanner. "Not everyone wants to talk about the past."

Sitting beside Tanner, Clementine paused in making silly faces at Boone. "We'd just like to get to know

Genevieve better, that's all."

"You can get to know someone," Ryder growled, "without pestering them to talk about their past."

Tanner sat forward, the tension in his body growing more visible. "Not everyone is against bringing up past events. In fact, some people actually like discussing it."

Ryder shoved back from the table and stood. "So that's what this is. You're trying to badger me again?"

Tanner was on his feet in the next instant, all charm gone from his expression, replaced by frustration. "All I need is our family name, Ryder. Just the family name. You can give me that. I deserve it."

Ryder shook his head and began to round the table, veering toward the door. "I knew I shouldn't have stayed."

"You can't avoid me and the past forever."

Ryder stopped next to Clementine. "We're leaving. Thank you for supper."

Clementine nodded. "I'm glad you came."

Genevieve rose, not quite certain what to do. The others were watching the two brothers warily, probably had witnessed the fighting on previous occasions, because this clearly wasn't the first conflict.

Before Ryder could take Boone from Clementine, Tanner jabbed Ryder's arm. "You're a coward."

Ryder swung back at Tanner, his hit harder and sending Tanner against a cabinet, causing the dishes inside to clatter.

Maverick jumped up from his chair. "C'mon now, fellas."

Tanner thrust away from the cabinet, his brows furrowing above rapidly darkening eyes. "I'm tired of you treating me this way, Ryder."

In the next instant, Tanner rushed forward and dropped his shoulder into Ryder's gut. The force sent Ryder backward, slamming him into the wall. A portrait of a happy couple fell to the floor, the glass frame shattering.

"Stop!" Clementine shouted.

Startled at the noise, Boone's arms flailed, and he released a piercing wail.

But all the attention was still fixed upon Tanner and Ryder. Tanner lunged at Ryder and threw a punch into Ryder's jaw, then another against his nose. Ryder's fists were clenched at his sides, and this time he made no move to fight his brother back.

"That's enough!" Maverick latched on to Tanner and hauled him away from Ryder.

Breathing hard and muttering under his breath, Tanner allowed Maverick to lock his arms behind his back.

Ryder remained against the wall, blood dribbling from his nose. His gaze was still locked with Tanner's, and it was filled with frustration. Tanner's expression, on the other hand, was taut with anger.

Maverick jerked against Tanner's arm to hold him back. "Beating up Ryder ain't gonna solve the problems."

"He's left me with no choice." Tanner spat the words.

Ryder just shook his head, then stepped toward Clementine and picked up Boone, whose cries were escalating. He cradled the baby in one arm before circling around the table toward Genevieve. Though his face was hard and his back rigid, his hand on her arm was gentle as he began to guide her toward the door.

Clementine followed them outside and said goodbye. Ryder gave his sister a hug but otherwise didn't say anything in return and was silent for the ride home. By the time they reached the homestead valley and the cattle came into view, the sky was lavender and peach in the west above the jagged mountain heights. Long shadows surrounded the cabin and barn, and the last rays of sunlight glinted on the distant meadows, turning the dried grass to flaming amber.

Boone had settled down, the rocking of the ride having lulled him to sleep. As Genevieve took him from Ryder, she wanted to say something—anything—to express how sorry she was for all that had happened. She didn't know who was at fault for the conflict and suspected both brothers were being stubborn. But she did know Ryder hadn't wanted to fight back, that he'd restrained himself from hurting Tanner. And she was proud of him for it.

However, Ryder didn't give her the chance to speak and was already leading their mounts into the barn. Instead, she carried Boone to the house, readied him for bed, then fed him his last bottle of the day. Once he was finished and asleep in his cradle, she went through her nightly ritual of sponge bathing, donning the night gown she'd purchased in Independence, and then brushing her hair. She didn't do one hundred strokes the way Lenora had required. Instead, she did fifty. Because the number suited her.

With every passing day away from Lenora's control, Genevieve's energy and lifeblood flowed with more strength and vigor. Or maybe the fresh air, homegrown food, and clear creek water were reviving her.

Whatever it was, she absolutely loved the freedom of being on her own with only the baby needing her. And even that wasn't so demanding.

Yes, there were times when she felt out of place and insecure—like earlier in the day when she'd attempted to scrub laundry for the first time. But somehow she'd figured out the process, thankful that she'd had the occasion to watch Constance doing laundry for the orphans a time or two.

As she pulled back the covers on the bed, she hesitated. She didn't want to crawl in and go to sleep as she had the previous nights—not without first learning how Ryder was faring. Even if he didn't want to converse about the fight with his brother, she could assist with his bloody nose or scrub the blood out of his shirt. She could at least do that, couldn't she?

She warmed water on the stove in preparation. As she waited, she lowered herself into the rocker beside the stove and curled up.

She wasn't sure how much time had elapsed when she awoke to find Ryder gently lifting her out of the chair and situating her against his chest. As he started to carry her toward the bed, she released a breath of protest. "I have water heating and must doctor your wounds."

"I'm okay." His voice was soft, tender.

"Please allow me to do this for you, Ryder." She wiggled in an effort to make him put her down.

He paused halfway to the bed.

"It will only take a few minutes."

He stared ahead at the log wall, his jaw flexing. Then with a nod, he lowered her gently to her feet.

She guided him to the rocker and pushed him down. Thankfully, he didn't protest, and as she stood at the stove and poured some of the warm water into a basin, she could feel him watching her every move.

For a reason she didn't understand, his attention flustered her so that she spilled a little of the water. And as she carried the basin back to him and placed it on the barrel that served as a side table, she was afraid her hands would begin to tremble and that she might spill more water.

She dipped in the rag, soaked it with the warm water, then wrung it out. All the while, he continued to study her. As she finally lifted the rag and turned to face him, the warmth and reverence in his eyes sent flutters through her stomach.

This wasn't about her, though. He'd been hurt and had a terrible argument with his brother. He needed someone to comfort him, someone he could lean upon, someone who would support him. And she wanted to be that person.

"This might hurt a little," she whispered, bringing the rag to the dried blood above his lip and below his nose. Carefully, she wiped at the splotch.

He didn't flinch, didn't move, didn't even seem to be breathing.

She dabbed again, blotting up most of the blood. "Is that okay?"

He gave an almost imperceptible nod.

She shifted back to the bowl of water, rinsed the rag, and then after wringing it, she dabbed his upper lip, which was swollen and split and oozing blood. "This seems to be your worst injury."

He was so near that her knees were brushing against his, and she could feel the warmth of his breath against her fingertips. He'd discarded his hat when he'd come in, and his hair was wavy and messy, the way it got when he stuffed his fingers into it.

She was tempted to smooth it down. But that would be highly inappropriate, wouldn't it? Or would it be one more way to let him know she was here for him and wanted to help him?

She pressed against his lip more firmly, hoping to staunch the flow. "How's that?"

Instead of answering with words, he took the rag from her hand and set it in the basin. Before she could back away, he settled both of his hands upon her hips and drew her around so that she stood between his knees.

Her heart gave a wild thump. What was he doing?

He released a long sigh, then lowered his head so that his forehead touched her stomach. Although he still didn't say anything, she had the feeling he wanted to talk about Tanner and express his frustration.

That was what she wanted him to do, wasn't it? She couldn't very well back away from him and put a proper distance between them—not when he needed someone to listen.

His fingers upon her hips splayed and tightened. He'd touched her in bed accidentally a few times, mostly a brush of his leg or arm while shifting positions. Just that morning, his arm had ended up around her, but not for long. And his fingers had woven through strands of her hair on occasion.

Her body hadn't reacted to those brief encounters—at

least, not much.

But now? A strange pleasure tightened low in her abdomen. Was she growing attracted to Ryder?

She couldn't name exactly what it was about him that seemed to draw her in. He wasn't the polished and clean-shaven type she was accustomed to in her social circles. Regardless, he was still good-looking in his own way, with his brooding eyes, lean features, and muscular body.

She couldn't let herself be drawn in though. She'd made the resolution the first day she'd met him. It wouldn't be fair of her to let an attraction develop—not when she planned to return home after she was twenty-one and free of Lenora's guardianship. And it wouldn't be fair of him to pursue an attraction either—not when he'd told her he only wanted a mother for his baby.

Even so, she liked Ryder. And she was glad she did. Having an amiable relationship would make the coming months much easier.

She let herself relax, and she placed her hands upon his shoulders in what she hoped was nothing more than a consoling gesture—one she hoped would reassure him that if he wanted to express anything to her, she was willing to listen. She'd always listened to her papa, had always been there for him, so this was something she could do, something she was good at.

He rested his head more solidly against her, as if he understood she was there to help bear his burdens, that he didn't have to do it alone any longer.

11

"Tanner and me..." Ryder started but then stopped. Was he really ready to share this ugly part of his life with Genevieve?

He closed his eyes and breathed in the scent of rosewater that permeated her nightgown. He hadn't meant to reach for her, hadn't meant to draw her closer. But her tenderness in doctoring his face had loosened something inside him. He wasn't sure what. All he knew was that he needed to talk to her.

She squeezed his shoulders, as though to reassure him that he could share more.

"We've been orphans most of our lives, and I've accepted it. But Tanner hasn't. He wants to find out who our parents were."

"I gathered he expects you to provide names for him."

"I don't remember the names, and I've told him that."

She was silent a moment. "The orphanage you were at would likely have records. At least, Open Door kept meticulous records of each child that came in."

"The first orphanage named us after the cowboys that dropped us off."

"Then that does pose a problem."

How much more should he share with her? How much could he even verbalize? He forced out the little bit she deserved to hear. "I should remember more, since I was five when our parents were killed, but nothing's there, not even names. Only nightmares with images I don't understand."

"Oh, Ryder. I'm so sorry." Her whisper was filled with compassion.

"The two cowboys told the orphanage that they'd picked us up from a tribe of Kickapoo in Kansas. Apparently, the Kickapoo took care of us for a while after finding us among the wreckage of a wagon train that had been attacked, but the cowboys didn't know much more than that."

She didn't say anything, just shifted one of her hands to his head. Somehow, that move eased the tension in his neck.

He rested against her for several heartbeats, then continued. "The past isn't important to me anymore. But for some reason, Tanner won't let it go."

Her fingers lightly teased his hair. "If he was younger

than you when everything happened, then he probably doesn't have the same nightmares haunting him."

"True."

"That means he doesn't have as much of a reason to let go of it." She combed her fingers into his hair deeper, still just as gentle.

He liked it a whole lot more than he should. In fact, he liked the way her hips curved beneath his hands. He liked the soft pressure of her stomach against his forehead. He liked the solidness of her body between his legs.

As her fingers threaded through his hair, he breathed out the last of the frustration that had built inside him since the moment he'd seen Tanner tonight. "I know it's important to him to find out, but I just can't help him."

"I understand." She paused in her combing.

He almost protested aloud. Instead, he tightened his grip on her hips.

"There are other ways for him to seek out family," she said. "I've seen orphans put advertisements in newspapers. Or he could investigate wagon train records from the year your family traveled west."

Ryder shrugged. "We have a life here and now. He needs to learn to be content with that."

She resumed her caressing of his hair. "I don't have anyone left, Ryder," she said hesitantly, a note of sorrow tingeing her voice. "You're blessed you have your brother."

Had he been focusing so much on the problems with Tanner that he'd started to take for granted the blessing that they were still together, especially when other people—like Genevieve—were completely alone?

He sat up, the move forcing her hands to drop to her sides. He didn't want her to stop combing his hair, but he wanted to see her face.

Her beautiful eyes were filled with the loneliness of someone who'd lost everyone she loved.

"I'm sorry." He knew he needed to let go of her too, but he couldn't force himself to do it. "I was insensitive and selfish."

"No, don't think on it—"

"I still have a brother. And I should be thankful for that." He needed to do better in all his interactions with Tanner. After all these years of battling hardships to stay together, he had to keep fighting for them, couldn't give up so easily—not after they'd come so far.

"I can see that you're a good man, Ryder Oakley." Her tone was as soft as her caress from moments ago had been. "And I believe you'll figure out a way to restore your relationship with Tanner."

She took a step back.

This time he had no choice but to break his hold of her hips. But he couldn't break his gaze, however. In her white nightgown, with the low lantern light casting a sheen on her long dark hair, she looked angelic.

Somehow, in this moment she seemed more real to him than anyone had felt in a long time, if ever. She'd listened, she'd cared, and she'd spoken truth into his hurt, not just telling him everything she thought he might want to hear but telling him what he needed to hear.

"And you, you're a good woman, Genevieve."

She visibly winced. Then she glanced away from him, as if she wanted to hide something—something from her past, something she was ashamed about. But what person—especially what orphan—was perfect and hadn't made messes of things at times?

He wasn't perfect. And he didn't expect her to be either. Before he could formulate the words to reassure her, she was already turning away and making her way toward the bed.

He wasn't ready for their time together to come to an end, but with the heat that was still churning inside him from having her hands in his hair, he guessed it was for the best to put an end to the intimate moment. He didn't want to get carried away and end up driving her out of his life. Because that's what he seemed to be good at doing— driving people he cared about away.

By the time he put out the light and climbed onto his side of the bed, she was already asleep. In just a few nights, he'd learned to tell when she was sleeping, because her breathing turned slow and deep and peaceful.

He liked listening to it. And he liked watching her

sleep, although he'd never admit as much to her. He rolled to his side, the moonlight sneaking past the slit in the curtains and illuminating her features, letting him admire each line and curve of her face.

After the angst that had been stirred up by the fight with Tanner, Ryder guessed the nightmares would be back in full force tonight, since most of them seemed to happen whenever he and Tanner fought.

Ryder situated his head on his arm more comfortably. At least if he woke up with one of his nightmares, he wouldn't entirely surprise Genevieve. She'd know now that he was haunted by a past he couldn't remember except for the vivid images that came all too readily to life in his dreams.

As his breathing evened out, he finally let his eyes close. Maybe he'd made a mistake in relegating his relationship with his new wife to a mere partnership rather than a real marriage. He could admit he'd partially done so to protect himself from more hurt after all that had happened with Sadie.

But what if he'd been too hasty in assuming that after one failed marriage, he'd never be able to find someone who would care about him or accept him with his faults? What if he'd been too hasty in dismissing the possibility that he could have a loving relationship like Pa and Ma Oakley?

Because he was starting to wonder whether, if he put

forth the effort, he might have something special with Genevieve after all.

The only way to tell was to give their relationship a chance to grow. What did he have to lose by doing that?

12

Genevieve pressed the silk scarf to her nose and breathed it in, never having imagined she'd miss shopping so much. But now that she was in the general store, she couldn't deny that she had missed the ability to shop whenever she wanted—even if purchases had been regulated by Lenora.

Genevieve fingered the silk. She'd managed to stay out of the public for three weeks and had lived on Ryder's ranch without going anywhere except to his family's home that disastrous evening for supper.

Not that Ryder hadn't offered to take her places, because he'd asked each week if she wanted to ride with him to get mail and supplies. He'd offered to take her to church, and he'd even asked if she wanted to go to a choir concert one Saturday evening.

She'd longed to acquiesce to each of his requests, had been ready for a taste of civilization after the solitude in the wilderness with a baby and a rancher. Not that she wasn't content with Boone and Ryder. She truly was satisfied with her situation, was growing very fond of Boone, and respected Ryder for how hard he worked.

Thankfully, Clementine had visited a couple of times and had helped her with harvesting and canning the vegetables and fruit for the coming winter. Each time, the task had been grueling and had taken most of the day. But in the end Genevieve had been proud of herself for persevering, especially when she'd taken stock of all the jars that lined the cellar shelves—jars of beans, peas, corn, tomatoes, plums, peaches, and more.

Clementine had been a delight to get to know—was vivacious and witty and entertaining. She'd also been a kind and patient instructor, answering all Genevieve's questions but also sharing more about the Oakley family—the details a man wouldn't think to reveal but that Genevieve loved learning, like how sweet their pa had always been to their ma, doing everything for her, giving her anything she wanted, and treating her as if she were a princess.

That revelation alone had helped her understand where Ryder had learned to be so attentive. Even though he'd been busy with haying, he'd made sure she was well taken care of, had all the supplies she needed, and was never overworked.

In spite of Ryder's unending work with running the

ranch, she felt as though she was getting to know him, that he wasn't a stranger anymore. They'd gone on a couple of hikes into the foothills. She'd accompanied him fishing on several occasions. And he'd taken her to pick serviceberries and raspberries, showing her how to tell the difference between berries that were edible and those that were poisonous.

Most days, however, they were both occupied with their own responsibilities. After a busy day, she was surprised at how much she looked forward to the evenings together. They'd fallen into the routine of eating supper, taking care of Boone, and finishing out the final hour with Ryder reading aloud from one of his books.

He hadn't talked any more about his past or Tanner, but for a few nights after the fight, his thrashing and strangled cries had awoken her. Each time, she'd reached over and brushed his hair off his forehead until he quieted and fell into a peaceful sleep.

Most of all, she loved the early mornings when they lingered in bed and whispered about their plans for the day or the new things Boone was starting to do or the news that they'd read in the newspaper he brought back from town.

She hadn't seen any other articles about the missing heiress, so this afternoon, when Ryder had asked again if she wanted to accompany him into town, she'd agreed.

"That scarf would sure be pretty on you." Mr. Worth,

the middle-aged store owner behind the counter, offered her a charming smile.

"It would indeed." She lowered it back to the counter and let her fingers trail over the royal-blue material, which wasn't as fine as the Parisian silk she was accustomed to but was still nice nonetheless.

"I'm good at leaving hints for husbands when it comes to gift giving." The store proprietor winked. "Do you have a birthday coming up?"

She shook her head. "No, not until next summer." If only it weren't so far away.

"Then come December, it'll make a real pretty Christmas present."

Balancing Boone in one arm, she pressed against her chatelaine with her free hand. She still had plenty of cash from when she'd sold the piece of jewelry in Denver, since she hadn't used any since arriving. She'd thought to simply purchase the scarf today and anything else that suited her fancy. In fact, she had already started a short stack of items she intended to purchase on the counter. One was a history book about the Middle Ages for Ryder, which she'd located among the smattering of books the store had for sale. She'd also picked out several small toys for Boone that would keep him occupied.

But if she pulled out her supply of money and made the purchase today, would she draw suspicion? Would the store owner and all the other customers wonder how she could afford such items?

They most certainly would if she bought the scarf. Because apparently women didn't buy scarves for themselves in the West. Apparently, they waited for birthdays or Christmas to receive such items as gifts. Or at least, impoverished rancher wives waited.

During the past hour or so of wandering among the stores on Main Street, she'd noticed several matrons who appeared to be ladies of some means. Although their garments weren't as stylish or finely made as those she'd always worn, the ladies had been fashionable enough to stand apart from the poor working women.

Obviously, now that she was married to Ryder, she was one of those poor working women.

She smiled at the store owner, the same proprietor who allowed Clementine to sell her candy in his shop. Although Clementine wasn't in the store at the moment, most of her gourmet candy was beautifully arranged on fine platters in a glass display case.

Genevieve had been impressed from the first moment she'd eaten Clementine's candy. It was more delicious than anything she'd ever tasted in the big cities. In fact, she'd wanted to tell Clementine that she could sell her candy in New York City and make a fortune doing so. But such a suggestion would draw unwanted questions, because a destitute orphanage worker wouldn't have the luxury of sampling the best candy in the city.

"Please do give Ryder the hint for Christmas," she said to Mr. Worth. "In the meantime, I would like to purchase the history book for him and three toys for Boone."

The man's smile faltered. "Today?"

"Yes, of course."

Boone was already holding one of the toys—a noisy rattle—and he shook it as if to agree with her.

"I will also buy a dozen pieces of candy." She may as well support Clementine. It would be the kind thing to do, especially after Clementine had explained how much work went into the different batches of sugary treats.

The store owner's brows rose. "A dozen?"

The other customers around her had ceased their shopping and were watching her. What had she done wrong? Was asking for the candy too extravagant? "You're right." She forced a smile. "I shall forego the candy today. Perhaps next time."

"That's probably wise." Mr. Worth's voice lowered to a whisper that only she could hear. "Ryder's tab is already quite high. I trust he'll pay it off once his hay is sold, but still . . ."

Her fingers were already opening the drawstring of her chatelaine. "Have no worries, Mr. Worth. I intend to pay for everything myself." She felt for one of the bank notes.

"It's no trouble to add it to the tab . . ."

As she laid the money on the counter, his voice trailed off, and his eyes rounded.

She glanced down to find one of her twenty-dollar bills. "Surely this is more than enough to cover the cost of my purchases."

"Yes, of course, but . . ." His eyes held a dozen questions, and no doubt one of them was where a woman like her had gotten such money.

She didn't want to lie any more than she already had, but she had to offer some explanation. "I do have a little remaining from my life in New York City." Her statement was partially true. She had much more than a little, though. The few remaining jewels she'd brought with her were some of the finest in the country, and a reputable jeweler would recognize that and give her what they were worth—thousands of dollars.

Mr. Worth stared at the twenty-dollar bill a moment longer before picking it up.

"Perhaps you can apply the remainder to Ryder's— our—store tab?" She had the feeling Ryder wouldn't approve, but it seemed like the least she could do to help with the extra expenses that came with her living on the ranch.

Her suggestion seemed to fluster Mr. Worth even more, but he did as she asked, nearly clearing Ryder's debt. Several minutes later, she stepped out of the store, carrying her new purchases in one arm and Boone in the other.

The afternoon sunshine wasn't as warm as it had been just a few weeks ago. The nip in the air was the reminder winter came early to the high country.

She hadn't brought a heavy coat or cloak with her and would need to purchase one soon. Every time she spent her money, would she face the same scrutiny from the store owner and others? She hadn't considered such a dilemma before today and hoped her purchases wouldn't cause people to question her true identity and link her to the lost heiress of New York City.

For the time being, she would have to be more careful.

She hefted Boone higher and started down the boardwalk in the direction of the wagon they'd ridden in. The town was growing busier with the passing of the afternoon, with more people milling about as well as additional traffic on the wide dirt road that ran the length of the town.

Breckenridge was larger than Frisco, with not only the central street containing businesses but also the side roads. Ryder had explained that the newly discovered silver veins in some of the surrounding mines were drawing more people to the area and that the town was trying to keep up with the growth.

Although Breckenridge might be bigger and more established than other mountain towns, most of the buildings were small with worn and weathered boards, the paint peeling on some, the windows dusty, and many of the signs hand-painted and crudely made.

Ryder had told her he had to get several tools sharpened and that he'd be at the blacksmith's, which was next to the livery. It was a wide rectangular structure with double doors large enough for a team and wagon to pass through. A tall brick chimney rose from the back, the smoke billowing out in an endless stream.

Though the interior of the shop was dark, she was able to distinguish an enormous bellows hanging from the ceiling and projecting toward a large brick oven. Several men stood together at what appeared to be a workbench, and she immediately recognized the broad shoulders and rugged build of the man with his arms crossed.

Even from a distance, Ryder was easy to spot. His presence was large and gruff and overpowering, but that tough aura only made him all the more attractive.

Her stomach gave a small flip as if to agree with her assessment.

He shifted so that he was facing the door. While she couldn't see his expression or features, she had the distinct feeling he was watching her.

Was he ready to go already? He'd indicated she could take as long as she needed for shopping. But now, after browsing and making the small purchase, she realized she'd had her fill, and she was ready to return to the ranch and be with Ryder again.

She took a step toward the street, but a woman's voice from behind startled her. "You've got something that belongs to me."

Genevieve turned around to find a young woman exiting through a door with "Wild Whiskey Saloon" painted in bright red letters on a sign above it. In a striped, yellow gown with an out-of-date bell-shaped skirt, the woman was still striking, with mounds of curling blond hair on top of her head and falling in lovely ringlets around her neck. She had on too much rouge, but even that couldn't detract from her pretty features.

The woman's narrowed eyes seemed to be finding fault with every one of Genevieve's features. Did the woman recognize her?

It had been a mistake to come to town. It was still too soon and too risky.

"Pardon me. Do I know you, miss . . .?" Genevieve tried to keep her voice calm even though anxiety was spurting through her chest.

"I've been hearing plenty about you." The woman's gaze trailed over Genevieve's clothing.

Genevieve had done her best to keep her new garments fresh and clean, but she'd quickly learned just how difficult that was with both a baby and farm work to take care of.

The woman finished her scrutiny with a huff and a sharp edge of haughtiness. And jealousy.

Genevieve recognized jealousy because wherever she'd gone, women had always been jealous of her for one thing or another. And over the years, she'd learned to be confident and uncowering in return.

Perhaps she needed to do so on this occasion. She lifted her chin. "May I help you?"

"Yes, as a matter of fact, you can."

"How so?"

The woman sauntered across the boardwalk, continuing to stare at Genevieve, clearly trying to intimidate her. When she stopped only a foot away, she dropped her gaze to Boone. "You can give me my son."

Genevieve's heart plummeted to the bottom of her chest. Was this Ryder's first wife?

Although Ryder hadn't talked about his previous marriage, Clementine had told her everything there was to know—that the woman's name was Sadie, and that she had grown up in Breckenridge and was remarried to a saloon owner. Clementine hadn't held back any disdain for Sadie. First, the woman had abandoned Ryder a week into their marriage, and then, after Boone had been born, she'd threatened to dump the baby at an orphanage if Ryder didn't come and get him.

"Sadie." Ryder's call from across the street was hard and unfriendly. He'd exited the blacksmith's and was already weaving past a team and wagon lumbering by.

As Sadie shifted her attention to Ryder, Genevieve

glimpsed something in the woman's eyes. Was it interest? Was Sadie still attracted to Ryder? Even though she was divorced from him and married to someone else?

Ryder was at Genevieve's side in the next instant, and he was glowering at Sadie, his eyes dark and dangerous. "Leave Genevieve alone."

Sadie offered him a smile—one that was wide and full of welcome. "Was just introducing myself to her. Nothing wrong with that, is there?"

Genevieve's heart pinched with a strange protectiveness. Sadie had no right to Boone or Ryder. In fact, if what Clementine had said was true, Sadie had even left Ryder without a goodbye.

Ryder didn't smile back. "My new wife is none of your business." His fingers lightly skimmed the small of Genevieve's back, as if he wanted to place his hand there but also didn't want to overstep himself.

In this particular instance, however, she wanted him to overstep himself and put Sadie in her place. If that meant touching her back, so be it. In fact, she sidled closer so that her shoulder brushed his arm.

Sadie was watching their interaction with sharp eyes, and her smile faded. "Your new wife is my business . . . since she's got my son."

Ryder's body stiffened. "You didn't want him—"

"He's still my son, and I should have a say in who's taking care of him."

Genevieve straightened her spine with all the authority and class she'd ever been taught. "If you have doubts about my abilities to be Boone's mother, I invite you to visit me at the ranch so we might get acquainted."

"Maybe I will." Once again, Sadie scanned her critically as if she hoped to find a glaring fault.

"I hope you do. You'll see I only have Boone's best interests at heart."

"I doubt that." Sadie's tone contained an insinuation that had to do with Ryder.

Before Genevieve could reply, Ryder was already speaking. "You gave Boone up. That means you don't get a say."

"I gave him up at the time because I wasn't settled. But now I am." She cocked her head toward the saloon, where several men stood in the open doorway, watching the interaction. Other pedestrians had also halted around them and were staring. "So maybe I'll take him back and raise him myself."

"You can't have him back." Ryder's voice turned low and menacing.

Sadie fisted her hands on her hips. "I'm his ma."

The two glared at each other.

Genevieve didn't realize her grip on Boone had tightened until he gave a wail of protest.

The sound seemed to break through the tension between Sadie and Ryder. Genevieve bounced Boone and at the same time tried to quell the rapidly rising frustration inside. She could sense that Sadie didn't really want the baby, that what she really longed for was Ryder's attention.

"You're not his ma." Ryder lifted his shoulders and held himself at his full height. "Genevieve is his ma, and that's all there is to it." With that, he began to guide Genevieve away from Sadie, the pressure of his fingers on her back urging her to move with him in the direction of the wagon.

They only made it a few steps before Sadie's voice taunted them. "You're wrong. I *am* his ma, and I'm aiming to raise him now."

"Over my dead body," Ryder called without breaking his stride.

She released a scoffing laugh "There's no way you can keep him from me, Ryder."

Ryder halted, tossed her another scowl. "Don't you even try to take him."

"Or what?"

Ryder's fingers on Genevieve's back had started to shake. It was the only sign of weakness she'd witnessed from him during the entire exchange. "I'll hire a lawyer."

"I'll hire one too."

Ryder shook his head and started forward, tension rolling off him.

It wasn't until they were seated on the wagon bench

and heading out of town that Sadie finally stopped watching them and returned inside. Even then, Ryder sat rigidly without speaking.

Genevieve knew she couldn't say anything that would comfort him. At the moment, there was nothing that could alleviate his concerns or Sadie's threats. The only thing she could do was let him know that she was there for him and would help him in any way she could.

He was holding the reins with one hand and resting the other on his thigh, pressing it down hard, likely to keep it from trembling.

She reached over and laid her hand over the top of his.

The muscles in his hand flexed beneath hers.

Maybe he just wanted to be left alone right now and didn't want to be reminded that Sadie was stirring up trouble because of his new wife.

She started to lift her hand away, but without shifting his focus from the road ahead, he quickly captured her hand and settled it in his so that their palms pressed together.

A hum of anticipation coursed through her, but as soon as it did, she snuffed it to silence. She was comforting Ryder. That's all it was and all it could ever be.

13

He was going to lose Boone.

The thought twirled through Ryder's mind all evening like a funnel cloud, picking up debris and growing in intensity so that by the time he climbed into bed, his head ached from the pressure.

Genevieve's efforts to comfort him had been admirable, just like after his fistfight with Tanner. She'd held his hand on the ride home, and her touch had soothed him so that by the time they'd finally arrived back at the ranch, he'd stopped shaking.

When they'd sat down together for a simple supper of dried beef in a creamy sauce over biscuits, she'd attempted to initiate conversation with him about what had happened in town earlier with Sadie, but he hadn't been able to bring himself to discuss it.

Genevieve hadn't nagged him about it either. She'd simply changed the subject and taken the moment to give him a history book that she'd purchased for him in town, assuring him that she still had some money left from her trip west and had wanted to give it to him. He'd tried to be appreciative, had tried to distract himself by browsing through it, but his mind had kept replaying Sadie's threats to take Boone away from him.

Now that the storm inside him was raging, the fear of losing another person he loved—this time his very own son—made him nearly ill. He tried not to shift on the bed with his nervous energy, but sleep was evading him, and he got up to assure himself that Boone was still in his cradle.

Finally, after at least the third time checking on Boone, he returned as quietly as he could to his spot. As he did, Genevieve's delicate fingers brushed against his cheek. "Go to sleep, Ryder," she whispered. "I'll keep an ear open for Boone."

He nodded and started to speak, except that her fingers shifted from his cheek to his hair. The touch was so soothing he closed his eyes and released a tight breath. He didn't know what it was about her touch that was able to calm him, but within seconds, the soft combing had eased the ache in his head and chest.

He liked that she could sense when he needed comforting and that she didn't hold back out of self-consciousness. After living with her for the past weeks, he'd realized she was genuinely one of the nicest people he'd ever met. She was patient, kindhearted, hardworking, sweet with Boone, and generous. He actually couldn't think of a better person to spend his life with, and he wished he had the words to let her know how he was feeling.

But the words seemed to get lost someplace inside. "Thank you," he whispered, all he could think to say.

"You're welcome," she whispered back. "Now try to go to sleep."

With her gentle touch in his hair, his lids grew heavy until at last, the troubles of the world faded away.

He was resting peacefully, nearly asleep, when shouts and gunshots erupted around him. He found himself in the back of a covered wagon. The jolting of the ride came to an abrupt halt, and he could hear a man's deep voice calling out. "Hurry, get the boys into the hiding place."

A woman crawled in through the opening at the back of the wagon. She began shoving aside barrels and crates, then she clawed at the floorboards of the wagon bed. A moment later, she lifted one of them.

"Come on, darling." Ryder couldn't see her face, but her hands beckoned to him—hands that were always so gentle.

He had a hold on his brother's hand, and they climbed off the small bed.

Outside the wagon, more urgent shouting filled the air. And then a piercing war cry in a language he didn't understand.

The woman's hand began to shake, but her voice remained calm. "Down you go for a little game of hide and seek." She lowered him into a tight space between the floorboards that was so narrow he had to lie flat, and a moment later she placed his brother beside him.

Once they were both side by side, she knelt above the opening. Though he couldn't visualize her, he knew she was peering down at them. "You must stay here until your father or I come to get you. Do you understand, Edward?"

He nodded.

As a terrified scream echoed from nearby, the woman began to replace the board, her hands shaking so much that she could hardly hold it. She paused with only a crack and looked directly at him. "You must also keep Donny from making any sound."

Before he could nod, the board fell into place, leaving him and his brother in darkness except for the slit in one of the boards at the side of the wagon.

He could hear the woman shuffling above him. Then a moment later, she seemed to leave through the back of the wagon as the man called to her, telling her to hurry. She passed by the wagon, trailing her hand along the board where he and his brother were lying.

"Mommy?" his brother whispered.

"She'll be back soon." He took hold of his brother's hand. "Now we must be quiet for the rest of the game."

He had hardly uttered the words when a horse thundered past the woman—his mother. "No, please!" she cried out. "Please!"

Her cry was cut off, and in the next instant she fell hard against the wagon, then slid to the ground.

"Sarah!" came the frantic call of the man.

The war cries only grew louder, drowning out everything else, filling his head, pulsing through his blood, and sending chills down his body. But he lay silent and unmoving as his mother had instructed, the screams and gunshots tapering off until he could hear his own rapid breathing and heartbeat.

Through the slit in the wood, he caught glimpses of the wiry Natives with their bronzed skin and their colorful war paint and feathers.

The hiding place was sweltering in the heat of the summer day, and beside him, his brother was growing restless, probably just as hot.

"I want Mommy," came his brother's soft whine.

With the growing silence around the caravan of wagons, he pushed himself to his elbows, ready to be free from the confines himself. But at the sound of footsteps entering the wagon bed directly above them, he pressed a finger against his brother's lips and whispered, "The game's not over yet."

He peeked through the slit in the side of the wagon bed, and his gaze landed upon a man facedown in the dirt, blood staining his shirt and forming a pool on the ground by his side.

A scream pushed for release, but he swallowed it. He couldn't let it out, couldn't let anyone know he was there with his brother. He had to stay silent, had to keep his brother safe, had to stay undetected.

He squeezed his eyes shut and gulped in one breath after another. Tears wet his cheeks, but the screams and cries remained silent, buried deep inside. The pressure against his chest was unbearable, the air stifling, the confines too much to bear.

Before he could stop himself, he sat up, desperate for a breath.

The cool darkness of the night surrounded him, yet he was burning up and couldn't make his lungs work.

Frantically he shoved off the covers, wheezing and clawing, but for what, he didn't know.

"Ryder?" A soft voice broke through the terror in his mind, and gentle fingers grazed his back.

He jerked up and found himself standing on shaky legs, hardly able to hold himself upright.

"What's wrong?" the voice asked. "Are you having a nightmare?"

He had to get air into his lungs. With a strange desperation pulsing through him, he stumbled across the cabin, banging into the table and chairs before he made it to the door. He shoved at the latch, but it wouldn't unlock.

With a growl, he fumbled with it until it finally opened. A second later, he found himself careening outside and falling into the grass. As his knees hit the ground, the jarring seemed to clear both his mind and his airways. He dragged in a deep breath, his body shuddering as he did so.

He'd had another nightmare. But this one, unlike those in the past, had been more than just images and sounds and terror. It had been real, as if he'd been there reliving what had happened.

At a touch upon his shoulder, he tried to calm himself. He didn't want Genevieve to see him so weak and vulnerable. But before he could assure her that he was all right, she knelt beside him, her nightgown pooling around her.

He sucked in another breath, the cold air soothing his lungs and waking him up even more.

She reached for his hand and squeezed it.

The black sky was filled with thousands of stars so plentiful and full of light that he could see the worry in her expression as she watched him.

He took several more breaths, feeling his heart rate return to normal and his muscles relax. "I'm okay."

"It's okay if you're not." She brought his hand to her lap and caressed partway up his arm with her other hand.

"Edward." He had to say the name aloud before he forgot it. "And Donny."

"Edward and Donny." She repeated the names as if they were clues to a long-lost mystery.

Maybe they were.

There was one more name from his nightmare. What had it been? The woman's name. He didn't want to relive the nightmare, didn't want to experience the tragedy again. But he needed the name for Tanner's sake.

The man in the dream had yelled it.

Ryder closed his eyes and put himself back in the bottom of the wagon, peering through a crack at the woman passing by. The man had called her . . .

His eyes shot open. "Sarah." He shifted in the grass so that he was facing Genevieve.

Her eyes were wide and her expression serious as she listened to him.

"Sarah." He said the name again, testing it. It didn't have a familiar ring. But he wouldn't have used it or heard it often, would he?

"Are you remembering names from your past?"

He nodded. "I think my name was Edward and Tanner's was Donny. And I think my mother's was Sarah."

"That's wonderful, Ryder." She stroked his arm again as if she were still attempting to calm him.

He was fine now. But he liked her touch—liked it a lot.

"Does Edward sound familiar?" she asked.

He tried to make his mind go back to his childhood, to the days before the orphanages. But as with the other times, everything was blank. "I can't remember if I was called that or not. Or whether Tanner was called Donny."

"But it's something new." Her voice contained a note of hope. "It's information you can relay to Tanner."

"It's not much."

"It's more than you've been able to give him before."

"But why now?" What had brought these memories to life so vividly this time, when he'd never had a recollection during previous nightmares?

"Maybe it has something to do with Boone and what happened with Sadie?"

His muscles tightened at the remembrance of Sadie's threats. Maybe the fear of losing Boone had brought up the losses of his past.

Genevieve shivered, then released him and hugged her arms to herself.

"You're cold." He reached for her, and before he stopped to think, he was drawing her close.

She didn't hesitate or resist him. Instead, she curled into him, letting him surround her and lend her some of his warmth. Too late he realized he was bare-chested. But she didn't seem to mind that either and rested her head against him.

The air was nippy on his bare skin, and the dew in the grass was damp against his knees. He ought to help her get up, go back inside, and return to the covers where they would both be warm. But with her soft body so near his, he couldn't make himself let go. Instead, he wrapped his arms around her more fully, so that his warmth would surround her.

He had the feeling she was just comforting him, the same way she had when they'd ridden home from town earlier and she'd held his hand like a friend would. But a part of him wanted more than just her comfort and friendship. He wanted her to see him as a man, to be attracted to him the way other women often were.

Even though a voice in the back of his head started ringing warning bells, reminding him that he couldn't ask for more, he buried his nose into her hair and breathed her in. Her familiar rosewater scent enveloped him—the scent that often wafted to him in the night if she turned in her sleep. He loved the scent because it belonged to her.

A swell of emotion rose so swiftly inside him that he stopped breathing. Was he falling in love with Genevieve?

He'd never been in love before and didn't have anything to compare his feelings to—except for how he felt about Boone. The love he had for Boone defied anything else and was so strong that he'd die for his son.

What he was experiencing now with Genevieve resembled that. He was growing to cherish her and would protect her with his life if necessary. He appreciated so much about who she was. And there was no denying how much he revered her beauty. Every time he looked at her, as he'd been doing when he'd been in the livery and she'd stepped out of Worth's General Store, she made his heart stop beating with how stunning she was.

And now, in this moment, with all the emotions swirling together, he knew it was more than simple attraction. Desire had been there from the moment he'd first laid eyes on her. No, this was something bigger and more encompassing.

The question was, how did she feel about him? Was she beginning to care about him in a deeper way too? She hadn't given him any indication of that. She never flirted. Was never suggestive. Was never inappropriate.

In fact, she was proper in every manner of the word, so much so that he suspected she would never initiate anything no matter how she might feel about him.

If he wanted more to develop between them, he would have to make the first move. And he wasn't used to having to do that and didn't quite know what he should do. All he knew was that he wanted to express to her how much he cared.

"Are you thinking about your nightmare again?" Her soothing voice came from against his chest.

"No, not anymore."

"Then what's wrong?"

He forced himself to breathe normally. She was

perceptive—one of the many things he liked about her. Would she figure out he was falling in love with her soon enough without him having to say or do anything?

Just in case she needed a little nudging in that direction, he pressed a kiss against her head. The silkiness of her hair against his lips only made him want to kiss her again. He bent in again, this time kissing her harder and longer.

He heard her breathing hitch.

What was she thinking? Was she trying to figure out how to pull away from him without hurting his feelings?

Maybe it was for the best if he didn't allow himself to get caught up in a physical relationship as he had in the past. He didn't want that to be his focus, had already resolved with this marriage he'd be different.

In order to be an honorable man, he had to release her and use the restraint he'd been developing at night sleeping next to her.

He began to sit back, loosening his arms from around her, but before he could let go, her lips grazed his chest, softly, tentatively.

The heat he'd carefully been keeping banked flared into flames, spreading through his body.

Even so, he stilled, held himself motionless. Had her touch been accidental? Or had she purposefully kissed him?

She didn't move either except for her breathing

growing more rapid, the warmth skimming his chest. It seemed to tease him with all the possibilities and closeness he could have with her. It was within reach, so close, so available. How could he turn her offering away, if that's what it was?

14

She'd kissed Ryder's chest. What kind of woman was she becoming?

Mortification pummeled Genevieve, freezing her to the spot in Ryder's arms.

With every passing day, she'd noticed herself growing more comfortable around him, so that earlier in the day, during the ride home from town, she'd thought nothing of laying her hand on his.

But that had been to console him, hadn't it? And what about moments ago when she'd started rubbing his arm? That had been to console him too, hadn't it?

Or was it more? The warm pleasure swirling around her abdomen felt like something more, but since she'd never had such sensations before—except with him—she wasn't entirely sure what those sensations meant.

What she did know was that she liked being in his arms this way and wasn't ready for him to let go of her quite yet. That was the only reason she'd initiated the kiss . . . and because he'd kissed her head first. If he could kiss her head, why couldn't she kiss his chest?

Her cheek lay flat against his hard muscles, his skin so warm and his flesh so taut. She hadn't hugged him in return, and her hands rested lightly on his bare arms. But she could still feel the power radiating from him and had the urge to wrap her arms around him and skim her fingers over the hard length of his back.

Why was she thinking such brazen thoughts? Was it because she'd secretly been admiring his perfect chest every night for the past three weeks? Even though she'd tried not to look at his bare upper half when they lay in bed together, she'd clearly looked more than she should have.

Her face flushed, and she was suddenly glad for the darkness that was hiding her reaction to him.

He shifted as though to move away again, and this time her arms slid around his waist as if they had a mind of their own.

He paused again for several heartbeats.

Oh dear. What must he think of her? She was being too forward.

She released him and sat back. "I apologize, Ryder—"

He lifted her and deposited her on his bent knees, so that now she was even closer to him.

She was on Ryder's lap. Just the thought shot a

strange heat into her blood—a heat that was different than the warmth in her stomach moments ago. This heat was thick and rich and sluggish, melting her body with each spurt of her pulse.

He seemed to hesitate, then he brought a hand up and swept the hair away from her cheek. In the process, his fingers caressed her skin, making her shiver, but not from the cold this time. He brushed back her hair again, dropping lower and grazing her neck.

All the while, his gaze was caressing her too, so that she was utterly lost in his eyes and the sensations he was awakening inside her—sensations that had fluttered to life before but were now roused altogether and clamoring for more of his touch.

Yes, she wanted him to touch her, wanted him to hold her, wanted him to kiss her again, this time on her mouth. She knew she shouldn't feel this way, but after the closeness they'd developed, she suddenly wanted more, much more.

His fingers slid through her hair to the back of her neck. As the gentle pressure there guided her head closer to his, he dipped forward too, angling his mouth toward hers. He halted an inch or so away, and she wanted to huff out her impatience and her need to kiss him. But she was inexperienced, had never done anything even remotely like this, and wasn't sure what came next.

He waited, as though seeking her permission.

Whether or not she ought to give it to him, she did. She lifted her chin, offering him better access to her mouth.

With her lips nearly touching his, she'd made it clear enough that she would kiss him. And a man like Ryder Oakley didn't need another invitation. He closed the distance and fused his mouth to hers with a powerful surge that knocked into her, swept her away, and carried her up to the clouds, where the world disappeared and all that existed was this man.

This man. His kiss wasn't at all tender. Not that she'd expected something chaste and proper from Ryder, because he was neither chaste nor proper. He was all desire and heat. And as his mouth moved against hers, he gave her no choice but to respond with the same desire and heat, so that she was kissing him back with a fervor that was almost shocking.

But the truth was, she wanted the deeper connection with him, had been longing for it, even though she hadn't dared to admit it. In this moment, she didn't want to think about the repercussions. She simply needed to feel this delicious passion swelling inside. And she wanted him to know how much she'd grown to admire him.

He shifted, and the kiss slowed its desperate tangle. Perhaps he'd realized his fervor and intended to pull away and bring the intimate moment to an end.

But she didn't want it to come to an end. Not yet. So

instead of letting him back away, she snaked her arms around his neck and pressed in.

He released a low groan, one that rumbled against her lips and echoed all the way to her soul. Then he dragged her closer and devoured her again, as if he couldn't get enough, not even if he kissed her every night for the rest of her life.

But that was the trouble, wasn't it? She wasn't staying in Colorado for the rest of her life and most certainly didn't belong on a remote ranch up in the mountains. While she was learning a lot and making the most of her time here, she would never be able to live in the West on the ranch permanently. It simply wasn't the life she wanted or had dreamed of having.

In addition, and more importantly, their whole marriage was based on a lie. She couldn't forget that.

At the thought of her deception, panic began to swell in her chest. What was she doing? By kissing Ryder, she was crossing boundaries she shouldn't have crossed.

She had to stop so that she didn't end up hurting him. He'd already been wounded by one wife, and she couldn't bear the thought of causing him more pain.

With a new force of desperation—this one born out of the need to protect this tenderhearted man—she pushed back, breaking the kiss and breaking her hold around his neck. She scrambled away, needing to put distance between them.

He held on to her for a moment, as though sensing her panic and not wanting to lose her. But as she struggled again to free herself, he let go, because he wasn't the kind of man who would ever force her to stay with him. Not for a kiss and not for her future.

She quickly rose to her feet, and only then realized she was breathing hard. "I apologize, Ryder," she managed. "We shouldn't have kissed."

"Nothing wrong with it." His voice was low and breathless too. He didn't move from the ground and instead peered up at her with dark, half-lidded eyes that made her want to throw herself down on his lap and allow him to keep on kissing her.

But she couldn't. Because regardless of what he said, there was something wrong with kissing him. "I cannot . . ." What excuse could she offer that would make any sense? Was it time to tell him the truth? The truth that she should have revealed from the beginning? That she wasn't Constance Franklin, and their marriage was only temporary?

He sat back on his heels. "Reckon we can change the nature of our marriage if we both agree to it."

She wasn't used to talking so frankly with a man—or anyone, for that matter—about the intimacies of a relationship. So the flush that had been present during their kiss flamed hotter. She couldn't even begin to imagine what their relationship might be like if she allowed herself to fall for Ryder—really fall for him.

But falling in love with him wasn't part of the plan. At least, not now. And she couldn't foresee them ever being truly compatible. "I cannot agree to it, Ryder."

He watched her a moment longer as though waiting for an explanation. When she didn't give one, he nodded. "Okay."

Was he really okay with her decision?

She didn't wait to find out. Instead, she spun and retraced her steps to the cabin. Once inside, she crawled back into bed, pulled the covers high, and faced away from Ryder's side. But even as she closed her eyes and tried to go back to sleep, the only thought racing through her mind was that she'd loved kissing Ryder and wanted to do it again, even though she knew it would only lead to heartache.

15

Hopefully Tanner was home.

Ryder reined in at the top of a rise and peered down into Arapahoe Valley where Eagle's Nest Lake spread out with its deep blue water the same color as the evening sky overhead. The glassy surface was so calm and clear that it reflected the tall ponderosa pines growing along the banks.

Although the view was as heavenly as always, Ryder didn't take the time to enjoy the beauty.

Instead, he nudged his horse down the rocky trail toward the log cabin that bordered the lake's western edge. He caught a glimpse of the well-constructed and solidly chinked structure in a slight clearing amidst the pines, but he didn't see any sign of his brother at the late hour or any smoke rising from the stovepipe that jutted out of the log beams of the roof.

It was possible Tanner wasn't there, had taken a trail-guide job for tourists or another group who needed an experienced mountain man to hunt for them or guide them to their destination.

But several miners down by One-legged Joe's Mine claimed to have seen Tanner out checking his traps yesterday. With September having arrived, marmot season had started. Since it was followed by grouse trapping in October, Ryder suspected Tanner would stay close to his home.

Over the four days since the nightmare, nothing more had come to Ryder—no other names or memories. But at least he had something he could finally give Tanner.

Now that the haying was done, he had a couple of weeks before the wheat was ready for harvesting. After that, it wouldn't be long before the cattle breeding season began, and he sold off some of his heartiest steers.

The truth was, his schedule was free enough to allow him a day or two to track Tanner down, and he wanted to find his brother and tell him the news about the names. It might not be enough for Tanner to use in his investigations, but at least he would know more than he had before.

Besides, it was past time to repair their relationship. Genevieve had been right that he was blessed to still have Tanner when some orphans had no one left.

"You better be home," Ryder grumbled as the horse slipped on the gravelly path. He rapidly righted the horse's footing and slowed down. He didn't want to get hurt and be delayed in returning to the ranch. Already, he dreaded leaving Genevieve and Boone for one night, and he wouldn't be able to stay away from them longer than that.

Thankfully, when Ryder had told Maverick about the names he'd remembered after his recent nightmare, his adoptive brother had offered to send Ross, one of his most trustworthy hired hands, to the ranch to watch over the place and do chores while Ryder rode out and found Tanner. Ryder had left a hammock up in one of the barn stalls for the fellow—the hammock that he'd been sleeping in for the past few nights since he'd kissed Genevieve.

Genevieve hadn't kicked him out of the bed in any spoken words, but she'd quickly shut down the possibility of allowing their relationship to develop into more. He'd tried to tell himself she just needed more time. After all, they'd only been together for about a month. And even though his feelings had escalated quickly, he couldn't expect that hers would.

He reminded himself again that he had to be patient. And that's why he'd refrained from joining her in the bed. He could hardly keep from reaching for her when she was within arm's length, much less lying beside him. Even before kissing her, his hands had sometimes strayed her way. But now, after the kisses . . . he had the feeling he'd stray even more.

And he was burning up with the need to kiss her again.

He closed his eyes briefly as a swell of desire pulsed through him. He'd loved the way her body had melded against him, how her arms had wrapped around him, and the way her lips had fit with his. She'd started tentatively, but her kiss had rapidly matched his with a burning fervor that had consumed him so that the world could have ended around him and he wouldn't have noticed.

Her passion had surprised him and still did. For a woman so composed and poised, she'd lost herself in the kiss the same way he had—or at least she'd seemed to.

So what had happened to put an end to the kiss and cause her to shut down the possibility of more between them?

He hadn't been able to figure that out over the past few days. He'd wanted to ask her, but it seemed like an odd question to bring up. After all, he'd been the one to suggest a partnership rather than a real marriage. Just because he was already changing his mind about what he wanted didn't mean she would.

He could only hope that eventually she would accept more to their relationship than a marriage of convenience. But a strange anxiety had plagued him ever since she'd walked away from him that night—an anxiety he hadn't been able to shake off, that had made him hesitant to leave the ranch.

As the trail leveled off onto even ground, Ryder directed his horse around the lake to the west. He stayed clear of the area where he suspected Tanner had his traps set, until at last he rounded a secluded corner of the lake, and the cabin came into sight again.

Tanner had strung lines between trees and built a few racks for all the furs that he was preserving. Most of them were the rusty-brown marmot skins. But other animals were mixed in—one fox, a coyote, and several hares.

Though the era of growing wealthy from fur trapping was long over, there was still a market, especially among wealthy easterners. Tanner had done well for himself over the past few years of trapping and selling his furs. Although he never spoke of the financial details specifically, it had apparently been enough for him to hire an investigator to help him try to locate family.

Ryder had never been all that happy about Tanner's wandering ways—had wanted him to stay close so he could keep an eye on him. But in one of their first fights after Pa Oakley's death, Tanner had shouted that Ryder had smothered him with all his worry and that he couldn't stand being around him and had to get away.

Tanner never seemed to mind the rough living of the wilderness. In fact, he seemed more at home in the mountains than anywhere else.

A small shed behind the cabin was locked, likely

containing pelts ready to be sold. A dugout canoe was propped against the shed along with paddles. A pair of long skis hung from the other side of the shed. But the lean-to shed was empty of Tanner's horse.

Ryder hesitated even getting down since it was clear Tanner wasn't there. Sunset was still a couple of hours away. If he turned around and left right away, he might be able to make it out of the mountains and back down into the Blue River Valley before the way grew too treacherous in the dark.

He wouldn't mind getting home to Genevieve and Boone, even if it was late. He sighed. Who was he fooling? Not only wouldn't he mind it, but he was eager to be with them again after being gone for the day.

He scanned the area one more time, taking in the cold fire pit near the shore, the carcass of a fish, and the distant bird of prey circling over the lake—probably one of the eagles that nested in the area.

Before he could shift his horse back around, the crackling of twigs in the woodland put him on alert. He surveyed the dense trees, his revolver out and his finger on the trigger. There was no telling what kind of trouble or wild animals lurked in the mountains, and he always liked to be ready for anything.

"What do you want?" called a voice from within the dense foliage.

It was Tanner.

Releasing the tension inside, Ryder stuffed his revolver back into the holster. "Hello to you too."

A moment later, his brother emerged from the forest, leading his mount. He wore his coonskin cap and a fringed leather buckskin coat. His face was covered with several days' worth of unshaven hair, but the hair couldn't hide the animosity in his expression.

Tanner didn't say anything until he halted halfway between the trees and the lean-to. "Why are you here?"

Ryder's mind went back to the nightmare. Although he couldn't picture Tanner's face any more than he could picture their mother's, his heart pinched at the remembrance of Tanner's soft whimpers for *Mommy*. He'd been too young to understand anything that had happened or why his whole life had been turned upside down.

"I had a nightmare this week," Ryder said.

Tanner shrugged. He was used to Ryder's nightmares, had grown up with them. But that didn't mean he had to be so callous and cold about it.

The usual words of irritation began to push up, but rather than start off their interactions with the antagonism that had been there for months, Ryder wanted this time to be different. *He* wanted to be different. "Listen, Tanner. I want to stop fighting—"

"I'm not fighting," Tanner stated belligerently. "I'm just trying to get information from you that you won't give because you're a stubborn coward."

Ryder swallowed hard, pushing down a defensive retort. Instead, he took a deep breath. "You're right. I have been a coward, and I'm sorry for not trying harder to help you with the investigation."

Tanner's mouth stalled around a response.

"I want to do better. And I think I can help."

His brother closed his mouth, then narrowed his eyes on Ryder. "What do you want?"

"I want us to be brothers again."

Tanner released a scoffing laugh.

"You're all I have left—"

"You don't know that."

Ryder kept his voice calm, even though the pressure inside was tight. "I pray that someday you'll find everything you hope to. But that won't change that I love you and don't want to lose you. Not now. Not after everything we went through together."

Tanner didn't immediately respond, seemed to be contemplating the declaration.

"I came out here to tell you about the details from the nightmare." Ryder hadn't shared anything in a long time. Tanner knew that.

At the statement, Tanner dropped the reins of his horse and stared at Ryder.

He wasn't sure how he'd finally gathered courage to talk about the past. Maybe it was because he'd already done so with Genevieve, and it hadn't seemed so terrible. Maybe because he was realizing that if he didn't change, he would lose Tanner, and he couldn't let that happen—not if it was within his power to make things right between them.

"This was the first one where, when I woke up, I actually remembered anything."

Hope flickered to life in Tanner's eyes. "Like real details and not a bunch of weird images?"

"Real details. Even names."

"What names?"

"Our mother's name was Sarah. I was called Edward, and you were named Donny."

Tanner whispered the names, likely trying to jar his own memory.

"I can't recall the name of our father or our surname," Ryder admitted, "but if this memory came back to me, maybe it will open the door now for more to return."

Tanner nodded.

Ryder slid down from his horse. "I'd like the chance to tell you the rest of the nightmare."

"Okay." The fighting edge was gone from Tanner's voice. In its place was something Ryder hadn't heard there in months. Peace.

Ryder nodded at his brother. Even if this new information would never bring any resolution to all that had once happened, hopefully it would help them both make peace with each other and with their past.

16

A strange despondency had plagued her all day.

Genevieve hiked slowly back to the cabin along the creek, the early evening sunshine warming her back. With Boone in the sling—which she'd been wearing from time to time—she had her hands free and had picked another small basket of blackberries.

"And no, I don't feel this way because of missing your father." He'd left early that morning after finishing his chores, and he wasn't due back until later tomorrow.

Something in her voice drew Boone's gaze, and he paused in chewing on one of the toys she'd bought for him—one specifically for teething babies. His brown eyes resembled Ryder's more with every passing day, as did his facial features and his expressions.

She smiled down at him and brushed a finger across his puckered forehead, hoping to convince him that everything was all right, even though her thoughts were churning.

The baby watched her for another moment before resuming gnawing at his toy.

Her heart swelled with love for Boone—more love than she'd thought could develop in such a short time. She'd been so naïve when she first arrived, when she'd believed she could keep from bonding with him. How had she ever thought such a thing possible? She supposed she'd been able to keep from getting too attached to the babies at the orphanage and had expected it would be the same here. But Boone had been all too easy to care about.

Additionally, she should have known herself—that she couldn't hold back from relationships, that she'd always loved people freely and generously. That's why Papa's death had left such a gaping hole in her heart. And that's why the growing aloofness with Lenora after Papa's death had been difficult to accept.

In spite of Lenora's coldness, Genevieve had hoped for the best—that Lenora would come to love her eventually, that they would get along, that Lenora could be family. Perhaps that's why Genevieve had been so quick to submit to Lenora's rules and control, because she'd wanted to win her over eventually. But of course, that hadn't happened, and the more control she'd given to Lenora, the more the woman had taken until it was all gone.

Genevieve paused at the last bend of the creek and breathed in the high-altitude air that she'd finally grown used to. The lowering slant of the sunlight turned the rippling water into jewels that rivaled those in her chatelaine. The light also splashed gold across the pines lining the banks.

As much as she appreciated the beauty and grandeur of the mountains and the ranch, she was growing more restless with every passing day. And today, with Ryder's absence, she'd felt that restlessness more keenly than ever.

Maybe the isolation was starting to bother her. After all, she wasn't accustomed to such a secluded life. She was used to the hustle and bustle of the busy city, the constant flow of people on the streets, even the ever-present servants in her homes.

Yes, that was it. The strange despondency of the day had more to do with missing her old life than missing Ryder.

Ryder had voiced reluctance with the plans to travel up into the mountains to find Tanner. But she'd assured him that she and Boone would be fine for a day or two, especially since he'd hired help to stay at the ranch during his absence.

Besides, it wasn't as if she spent all day every day with Ryder when he was home. In fact, both of them were usually busy with one chore or another. There had been entire days when he'd been out in the fields haying or rounding up the cattle or repairing fences and she'd only seen glimpses of him.

Even so, she supposed knowing he was close, or being able to see him from a distance, had kept her from missing him the same way she was today. Or maybe she just had to admit the longing for him had been steadily growing over the past month. Although she tried to deny it, the truth was that ever since the kiss, her yearning to be with him had increased to unbearable proportions so that he was never far from her thoughts during the day or at night.

Although his sleeping in the barn this past week had probably been for the best, his absence made the nights long and restless. And it made the awakening at dawn dismal and quiet.

As embarrassing as the topic was, she knew why he'd changed their sleeping arrangements. After sharing such passionate kisses after his nightmare, it would be all too easy to share more such kisses, especially in bed together. But because she'd indicated she didn't want their relationship to change, he was respecting her choice.

He was such an honorable man. And she loved that about him. But there had been times over the past few days when she'd wished he weren't so strong and would touch her or kiss her again.

Like after supper last night, when he'd helped clean up the meal. There had been one point when he'd stood behind her, close enough that she could hear his breathing. Her whole body had awakened to his nearness, to his warmth, to his manliness, and she'd wanted him to wrap his arms around her from behind and just hold her.

But he hadn't touched her. Instead, he'd stalked to the door, jammed his fingers in his hair, then left a moment later, and he'd stayed away the rest of the night.

"Oh, Ryder." She breathed out the longing that was tightening her muscles. "Why does this all have to be so hard?"

Should she try to figure out a way to stay with him after she turned twenty-one? To make the marriage real? To make their relationship last?

She peered around at the wilderness, the pines, and the mountain peaks. Even though this didn't feel like home yet, maybe it would eventually . . . if she gave it more time. If she put her mind to it, she could develop new passions, new endeavors, new charities in this new place, couldn't she? Surely she'd eventually grow accustomed to the simplicity and silence of the land.

She'd never thought she would consider living in Colorado on a ranch. But could she really leave him and Boone and return to another life? With the way she was feeling after only one month with them, how would she feel next summer after twelve months? Would it be impossible to separate?

Besides, wasn't it true that if you loved someone

enough, it didn't matter where you lived or what you did, as long as you were together?

Her pulse slowed to a halt. *Loved someone.* Did she love Ryder?

She shook her head. How could that be possible in such a short time? And yet, she'd never felt this way about anyone before, not even Prescott.

As the son of one of her papa's closest friends and business associates, Prescott had been one of Papa's top choices for a potential husband. Papa and Mr. Price had always been very open about the prospect.

A couple of years ago, not long after she'd turned eighteen and after she'd finally started to heal from losing Papa, Mr. Price had been the one to reacquaint her with Prescott and begin arranging visits and outings. She'd always liked Prescott when they'd been children, and she'd liked him even more as an adult. He'd been kind and chivalrous and attentive.

Of course, the visits and outings had all been under Lenora's strict supervision. But it hadn't mattered at the time, because Genevieve had enjoyed getting to know Prescott and had even begun to fancy herself marrying him. Her feelings had grown strong and his had too.

She'd believed he might even consider proposing to her. At that point, Lenora had revealed everything her private detective had learned about the Prices—that they were in financial trouble, several of their business endeavors had failed, and they were hoping to use Genevieve's dowry to ease the burden.

Genevieve had confronted Prescott. He'd been shocked by the accusations and had wanted to prove the findings weren't true by marrying her without a dowry and showing her that he didn't want or need her money.

Lenora, however, had insisted that Genevieve break off her relationship with Prescott and the Prices immediately or face consequences.

Choosing to believe Prescott, Genevieve had pushed forward with the courtship regardless of Lenora's threats. Not long after that, Lenora had taken matters into her own hands and made sure all of New York City learned about the Prices' financial disasters and struggling businesses. As a result, Lenora had ruined the Price family's reputation, and the Prices had lost most of their business in the east and been forced to move out of the state to avoid complete ruin.

Of course, Lenora had insisted she was acting in Genevieve's best interest, claimed Genevieve hadn't known all the facts, and accused Genevieve of thinking too much with her heart and not with her head.

Part of Genevieve wondered if Lenora had been right. Another part suspected her stepmother had sabotaged a perfectly fine relationship with Prescott. But why? Especially when Lenora had nothing to gain from doing so. Papa's will was ironclad, with the inheritance only belonging to Genevieve. The guardianship would soon come to an end, and after that, Lenora would be allowed to take the amount Papa had designated for her. So what did Lenora have to gain by keeping Genevieve from getting married to Prescott Price?

Her stepmother would probably like Ryder even less than Prescott. Ryder wasn't wealthy, didn't have a prestigious family, and wasn't a part of the same social circles. And yet, Genevieve had the feeling her papa would have liked him a great deal. He would have liked how direct and honest Ryder was. And he would have liked that Ryder was honorable and noble and was attempting to do the right thing with his life even after making mistakes.

"Oh, Papa," she whispered. "What should I do?" Even after four years, she still missed his wisdom and his practical outlook on life. He'd always been just as direct and honest as Ryder . . . and he would have been disappointed to learn how dishonest she'd been over the past weeks. He would have been disappointed that she hadn't been more forthright with Ryder. Maybe he even would have been disappointed that she hadn't been more forthright with Lenora, stood stronger against Lenora's tightening control.

Genevieve started around the slight bend in the river and up the final incline that led behind the cabin. With each step, her head hung lower and her heart felt heavier.

She knew exactly what her papa would say if he were here to share his wisdom. He would say to be like Ryder and correct her mistakes.

That meant she had to tell Ryder the truth about her real identity, about taking Constance Franklin's place and deceiving him into thinking she was someone she wasn't. No matter what the outcome, she had to stop living a lie.

The nerves in her stomach tightened. She didn't know what Ryder's response would be. But she needed to tell him before too much more time elapsed. Perhaps he'd understand and try to find a solution for their relationship that would be workable. Or maybe he'd be so angry he'd send her away and never want to see her again.

Regardless of Ryder's reaction or what might happen, it was past time to confess what she'd done and make amends.

As she reached the top of the creek bed and the back of the cabin came into view, the sound of approaching hoofbeats greeted her.

Her heart gave an extra beat. Was that Ryder returning already? Maybe he'd located Tanner right away, said what he needed to, and wouldn't have to be gone overnight after all.

She picked up her skirt and her pace. She rounded the cabin and made her way to the front but then halted abruptly at the sight of the three riders nearing the ranch yard. One was a woman wearing a bright blue gown that accentuated a curvy body, her blond hair piled high in fancy ringlets.

Sadie. Ryder's ex-wife.

Sucking in a sharp breath, Genevieve fell back into the shadows, out of sight. She waited several seconds until the hoofbeats tapered to silence. Then she peeked around the corner and took in the other two riders, both men.

One had to be Axe, Sadie's husband. In a light-blue suit that was too tight and a white straw hat that was at least a decade out of date, he was clearly trying to look the part of a gentleman.

But who was the other man? With a narrow face and pointed gray beard, he wore a tall black top hat and black suit and appeared to be a man of some importance.

Did Sadie's visit have something to do with the argument earlier in the week? The one where she'd threatened to take Boone away from Ryder and raise him? It wasn't as though Sadie didn't have a right to see her baby. And she even had a right to change her mind about raising him.

But after wanting nothing to do with Boone all along, why was Sadie having a change of heart now?

Genevieve suspected Sadie's jealousy was playing a role in it. When Ryder had been exhausted and struggling to raise Boone on his own, the young woman hadn't had a reason to be envious. But now that Ryder had a new wife and was happy, perhaps Sadie thought she was missing out on something.

Or maybe Sadie was the kind of woman who wanted all the attention on herself. Even if she didn't want Ryder anymore, perhaps she still wanted him to desire her.

Whatever the case, Genevieve couldn't think of any other reason why Sadie would be out here at the ranch unless it was to follow through on the threats she'd made to Ryder to get a lawyer and take Boone back.

Maybe the important-looking man was the lawyer.

"Where's Ryder?" Sadie called.

Genevieve hesitated. Had Sadie spotted her? Should she step out of the shadows and tell the woman to return on a different day, when Ryder was home?

At the lengthening silence, Genevieve sighed and started to step forward. She halted when Ross, the hired hand, called out an answer from the area around the barn. "He ain't here today. What can I do for you?"

"Came to get my baby."

A surge of possessiveness shot through Genevieve, and she wrapped her arms around the sling and Boone.

"Ryder said to start shooting if you came out and tried to take his son." At the echoing click of a rifle, it was clear the hired hand had taken Ryder's side of the dispute and not Sadie's.

Genevieve was on Ryder's side too, and she wouldn't even consider relinquishing Boone to Sadie today—not while Ryder was away and unable to fight for the child.

She glanced back the way she'd come. Should she run away and hide until Sadie was gone?

"I've brought my lawyer with me." Sadie's call had a note of confidence to it that made Genevieve back up a step.

She'd been right about the man's identity.

"Don't matter," came the hired hand's reply. "You'll have to come back when Ryder's here."

"Mr. Irving says the baby belongs with me," Sadie insisted. "The tender years law does too."

"Tender Years Doctrine," came a voice that presumably belonged to the lawyer, Mr. Irving. "It's not yet technically a law here in Colorado, but most courts are beginning to accept the rationale that a baby needs his mother most during the early years of his life."

Several beats of silence followed.

"If it ain't the law yet," the ranch hand finally said, "then reckon the baby is still Ryder's."

"It's only a matter of time," the lawyer cut in, "before a court will allow Sadie to have the baby."

"Yep," Sadie added. "May as well save us all the trouble and hand the baby over today."

Genevieve inched farther back, grateful to Ross for coming to Ryder's defense. Even so, she needed to go now, before Sadie decided to take matters into her own hands and search for Boone. If the baby wasn't there, then she wouldn't be able to take him.

Without waiting to hear any more of the conversation, Genevieve slipped around the cabin and made her way back toward the creek.

As she climbed down the trail that ran along the creek, her mind raced with the possibilities of everything that could happen, including Sadie and Axe and the lawyer pushing past the ranch hand in spite of his rifle and threats.

Maybe Sadie would decide that the only way she'd get Boone away from Ryder was if she came back later under the cover of darkness and stole him while Ryder was still away and wouldn't be there to stop her.

Or what if she returned with a judge or sheriff? How would Genevieve be able to protect Boone then?

No, she needed to locate a safe place to take Boone for a night or two, until Ryder returned and could put an end to the threats. Should she go to High Country Ranch and take refuge with Ryder's family? Or would that be the first place that Sadie would look for her and Boone?

As she circled around Ryder's ranch to the north, she found herself on the rocky trail that she'd used that first day she'd ridden out from Frisco with the livery owner. Her feet seemed to have a mind of their own, and she was soon rapidly hiking the two miles toward Frisco. Even though the shadows of the evening were lengthening, she guessed she still had time to make it into town before darkness fell.

Once she was there, she would take a room in a hotel for the night and work out a plan for making certain Ryder would never lose Boone. It was the least she could do for him.

17

Unease ate at Ryder's gut as he approached the ranch. Everything was too quiet for midday. And no one was in sight. Even the sun was hidden behind clouds, and rain had begun to spit for the last mile or so of his journey out of the mountains, so that eventually he'd had to stop and put on his oiled cloak.

He scanned the cabin for some sign of Genevieve and Boone, but the door was closed, the windows were dark, and there was no smoke curling from the chimney.

Where was Ross, Maverick's trusted ranch hand? On the ride in, Ryder hadn't seen him out by the cattle in the far pasture. He wasn't anywhere around the ranch yard. And if he was in the barn, why hadn't he come to the doorway to see who was approaching? Any good rancher knew he had to be alert just in case the visitor was on the wrong side of the law.

Instead of heading toward the barn to take care of his

horse, he veered in the direction of the cabin. He didn't know why he was worrying. Genevieve had never given him a reason to think she'd leave him the same way Sadie had. After a month, she hadn't made any mention about being discontent. She'd always seemed determined to make their living arrangement work. Above all, she was honest with him and would surely tell him if she were having second thoughts about staying.

Even with all the reassurances he'd been giving himself since starting the long ride back to the ranch this morning, the pressure had been mounting with each passing mile, so that he'd finally pushed his gelding into a gallop for the last of the distance.

There was even a part of him that wished he hadn't gone off at all, that scolded him for leaving her and giving her the chance to sneak away. But the other part of him—the rational side—reminded him he couldn't cling to her, or he might end up suffocating her and driving her away, the way he'd done with Tanner.

No, he'd been right to take the couple of days to visit his brother. Even if he'd gotten off to a rocky start with their conversation, the rest had been a satisfying time of reconnecting. They'd fished along the lake, cooked their catch over the open fire pit, and then reminisced for a while about their life with the Oakleys. Of course, they'd talked more about Ryder's nightmare and what it all might mean. Tanner had made a list of things to share with his investigator and had ridden part of the way out of the mountains with Ryder before branching off and going to Breckenridge to send a telegram.

Ryder hoped the conflict of recent months was now a thing of the past. But he also knew that in any sibling relationship, there would still be strain at times because no one was perfect.

The rain was falling steadily, pattering now against his Stetson and cloak and dripping to the ground. As he dismounted, he peered again through the windows of the cabin. Then, without a knock of hello, he shoved open the door, not caring when it banged against the wall.

The place was just as deserted as he'd thought. Even so, his gaze jumped directly to the spot underneath the bed, where she'd stowed her empty valise.

It was still there.

Her brush and mirror and soap were still on top of the chest of drawers where she kept them. Her extra pair of shoes sat beside the chest, her nightgown was folded next to her pillow, and one of her hats hung from a peg by the door.

He released a tense breath and leaned against the doorframe, relief weakening his legs.

Would he ever be able to trust again? Or had Sadie ruined him for any other woman?

With a growl of frustration toward Sadie, he pushed himself upright. He'd already given her enough power over his emotions and his life. It was time to let go of his failures and forge a new life with Genevieve—one where he wasn't constantly comparing her to Sadie.

He ducked out of the cabin, then led his horse to the barn. As he stepped inside, he listened for any signs of Genevieve or Ross. Except for the soft patter of rain on the roof and the snort of a horse in a nearby stall, the place was silent.

He swiped off his hat, ran his fingers through his damp hair, then slapped his hat back down. Where was everyone?

He stepped back into the open barn doorway, scanned the landscape through the drizzle, and finally caught sight of a couple of cowboys in the distance, riding up from the south and heading his way. After a moment, he recognized them—one was Maverick, and the other was Ross. And they were riding hard. Too hard.

Anxiety reared inside him again. Why did he always have to think the worst had happened? Why couldn't he be more relaxed? Surely there was a logical explanation for why Maverick and Ross were in a hurry and Genevieve wasn't home. After all, he was back earlier than he'd indicated to her yesterday, since both he and Tanner had been eager to get going at dawn.

He stepped out of the barn so that Maverick and Ross would be able to see him right away. And within a minute, they were reining in beside him, both of them soaked, their faces haggard, and their eyes brimming with remorse beneath the brims of their hats.

Something *had* happened. And it wasn't good.

"Well?" It was the only word he could get out.

Maverick slumped in his saddle. "It's Genevieve. We can't find her or Boone."

"She went on a hike up the creek yesterday," Ross added in a solemn voice. "And she never came back."

The world was beginning to spin around Ryder. She hadn't left him. He'd already concluded that. Otherwise, why wouldn't she have taken her bag and belongings?

Maverick began to dismount. "We've had a search party out most of the night and all day so far."

"And?" Ryder tried to draw in a breath, but he felt as though he were drowning. Was this really happening to him again? Was he losing someone else he loved?

Maybe he was cursed.

"And we haven't found her." Maverick's feet hit the ground, and he started toward Ryder, his brows furrowed.

Ryder held up a hand to hold Maverick back. He needed a few seconds to compose himself. But even as he tried, his mind spun with all the possibilities of what could have happened to her. Had someone kidnapped her and Boone? Had she gotten lost and fallen into a ravine? What if she'd been attacked by a wild animal? What if she'd taken shelter in an abandoned mine but then got trapped?

Maverick halted a few feet away, rain dribbling down his hat and cloak. "We think this might have something to do with Sadie."

"Sadie?"

"Yep." From atop his horse, Ross shook his head in frustration. "She came out to the ranch yesterday evening with Axe and the lawyer, claiming that she gets to have the baby. Course, everybody from here to Santa Fe knows that woman don't deserve the baby."

"What happened?" Ryder didn't care that his tone was harsh and demanding. All that mattered was finding Genevieve and Boone and making sure they were safe.

The cowhand patted his rifle in his saddle. "Told them they could eat lead before I let them have the baby."

"They left and went back to town," Maverick continued the tale, "but now with word of Boone and Genevieve being gone, people are saying that you hid them away so that Sadie can't get her hands on the baby." Maverick's brow lifted as though he was hoping that maybe there was a sliver of hope the gossip was true.

"No, I don't have them."

Ross nodded. "My only other guess is that she saw Sadie coming out to the ranch and ran off to keep the baby safe."

Ran off. The very words sliced into Ryder's heart. Even if Genevieve had only been trying to protect Boone, she'd run off without a word. She obviously didn't realize how her actions would worry him, didn't know how haunted he still was by all that had happened with Sadie.

Now, most likely she'd gotten herself into some kind of trouble out in the wilderness. If she'd been gone overnight and now half of today, they couldn't waste any more time. They needed to find her before another night set in.

Ryder was already stalking toward his horse, which was standing where he'd left it by the barn. He rapidly mounted, then dug in his heels, sending the horse into action.

Behind him, he could hear Maverick calling out instructions to Ross. A minute later, Maverick's horse easily fell into a gallop beside him. "Do you think you know where she went?"

"No, I don't. But I do know someone who can track her down."

"You heading back up into the mountains to get Tanner?"

Tanner was an expert tracker. Not even rain would be able to deter him from finding clues that would lead him to Genevieve and Boone. As desperate as Ryder was feeling, he would have gone right back up and begged his brother to come down and help him. But hopefully he'd find Tanner in Breckenridge, getting ready to send a telegram in the post office at the back of Worth's General Store.

He explained the situation to Maverick on the ride into town. Although Ryder wasn't normally a man of many words, he did his best to explain the information he'd given to Tanner and how he was attempting to repair their relationship.

Even though Ryder had parted with Tanner on friendly enough terms, they still weren't as close as they used to be. But Genevieve and Boone meant more to him than anything else, and he'd go to any lengths to find them, even if he had to tie Tanner up and drag him out to the ranch.

When they reached Worth's General Store, Tanner's horse was hitched out in front. Hopefully he was almost done composing his telegram, because Ryder needed him right away.

Ryder hopped down from his horse, and his feet barely hit the ground before the door of Wild Whiskey Saloon opened and Sadie stepped into the doorway in one of her fancy gowns. Although she glowered at him, she didn't chase him down, probably because she didn't want to get wet in the rain.

Ryder had never been happier for a rainy day. He didn't need to deal with Sadie now—not when the woman he loved and his baby were out somewhere in the wilderness and he needed to find them.

The woman he loved. The desperation in his chest pulsed even harder. Yes, he loved Genevieve more than he'd loved anyone, and he couldn't imagine his life without her in it.

He tried to ignore Sadie, but the rain didn't stop her from cupping her hands around her mouth and shouting at him. "Mr. Irving says you'll go to jail if you don't hand over the baby."

Of course, every other person on Main Street heard her and stopped to stare. At midday in the rain, there weren't many out. Thankfully.

Even so, Ryder's gut churned with the embarrassment that had been like a dark shadow following him around for the past months. If only he could put the scandal behind him and just go back to the ranch and live with Genevieve and Boone without any more problems.

But it was becoming clear Sadie wasn't about to let her claim on Boone go. He would have to find a lawyer of his own now to battle her for custody of Boone. He didn't intend to hand the boy over to her without a fight. A big fight, if necessary.

"Jail, Ryder!" Sadie shouted again. "You're going to jail if you don't give me my kid."

He stalked to the door of the general store with Maverick on his tail. He jerked the door open and stepped inside, only letting himself breathe again when the door closed and shut out her threats.

Clementine stood behind one of the counters, greeting him and Maverick with brows furrowed over her worried green eyes. "I already told Tanner he had to ride out to your place and help you track Genevieve and Boone. He said he would once he's done."

Ryder gave her a nod of thanks but didn't slow his pace as he stalked through the store, which wasn't all that busy, with only a few customers who had stopped their browsing to watch him. He should be used to all the attention, but he supposed he would never stop longing for the day when he could finally have a normal life.

Had he ever had normal? Maybe for the years he'd lived with the Oakleys. But even then, no matter how much they'd become his family, he'd always known he was different and that a piece of him was missing.

Did Tanner have that missing piece too? Was that why the investigation was so important to him? Maybe it would do them both good to fill in the gaps. Maybe it would bring about the healing they needed so that they could move on with their lives.

As he neared the back counter, Mr. Worth pushed aside the curtain that separated the store from the room with the post office. The usual welcoming smile was absent. Instead, his mouth was set in a grim line. "Was hoping I'd see you soon."

Ryder tapped at the counter. "Can I go on back and talk to Tanner?"

Mr. Worth shook his head. "Wanted to show you something first." He set a newspaper down on the counter.

"Don't have time." Ryder tried to peer through the slit in the curtain.

Mr. Worth slid the newspaper so that it was directly in front of Ryder. "It's about your wife. Genevieve."

Something in Mr. Worth's tone finally drew Ryder's attention. The man's eyes were filled with remorse . . . and pity?

Why?

Ryder lowered his gaze to the newspaper. *The Denver Daily Tribune.* The date was from the previous week, and the columns of articles didn't look any different than normal. Except one. The one Mr. Worth was pointing at.

The headline read: *Reward for the Return of Missing Millionaire Heiress, Elizabeth Genevieve Hollis.*

Ryder shook his head and tried to push the newspaper away. "This isn't my Genevieve."

Mr. Worth placed both hands on the newsprint to keep it flat and directly in front of Ryder. "Read the article."

Maverick was bending over the newspaper and began to read it aloud. "Miss Hollis disappeared from her home in New York City in early August and has been missing ever since. Five foot, three inches, long black hair, light blue eyes, pale skin, pretty features, and a slender build. Her loving family is seeking her return. Any information regarding her whereabouts is eligible for a reward."

With each word, Ryder's stomach began to cinch

tighter, so that when Maverick finished, Ryder read the article for himself silently a second time. Then a third.

He finally stood back from the counter. "This can't be her." Genevieve was an orphan who had lived and worked at Open Door Asylum. She wasn't a missing millionaire heiress with a family who loved her and was looking for her.

"I saw a notice a few weeks ago," Mr. Worth said in a low voice, clearly trying to keep their conversation personal.

Too late for that. Everyone in the store had likely heard Maverick read the article.

"I was wondering then about it," Mr. Worth continued. "But then when Genevieve came into the store earlier in the week, I put two and two together, especially when she opened her purse and pulled out a twenty-dollar bill from a pretty big wad of cash."

Her purse always had looked full and heavy. But Ryder had respected her privacy and hadn't prodded into the matter.

Maybe he should have. . . . Even from the start she'd indicated that she'd had no trouble paying for her fare to the West. She'd had more than enough to purchase new clothing. Maybe everything had been new. Her valise certainly was nice. And then, yes, she'd had money to buy him the book and Ryder the toys.

A poor orphanage worker likely wouldn't have had

that kind of money—not even if she'd saved for years.

"She's a real lady, that one," Mr. Worth was saying. "Can tell from the way she holds herself that she's no ordinary woman."

Ryder couldn't deny it. Genevieve had always moved and acted with a grace that set her apart. She'd been ignorant of so many tasks that most poor women knew how to do. And her hands had been too soft and unblemished, not those belonging to someone who had labored hard for years.

He'd seen all the signs that pointed to her being a wealthy heiress, but he'd been too enamored of her to question any of it. And he'd been too enamored to question the differences in appearance that hadn't matched up with the description in the letter he'd received from Constance Franklin.

How had Genevieve gotten his letter if she wasn't Constance Franklin? Had she worked with Constance Franklin at the orphanage, perhaps as a volunteer? Or maybe Constance Franklin wasn't even real.

A hard brick seemed to fall into the pit of Ryder's stomach. If Genevieve was the missing woman in the newspaper article, then she'd lied to him about everything. But why? Why had she done it? And what did she want?

The curtain pushed aside behind Mr. Worth, and Tanner slid through. From the seriousness of his expression and the questions in his eyes, it was clear he'd heard enough of the conversation to realize what was going on.

Ryder dropped his head, despair rolling through him. And embarrassment. He'd already had one marriage turn out bad. And now here he was again with another.

"Reckon we need to head on out." Tanner's voice held resignation.

Ryder wanted to yell out no, that Genevieve could stay lost for all he cared. But that wasn't the truth. He did still care. And that was the problem. He'd allowed himself to care too much about her. He hadn't wanted a wife, had wanted to keep the relationship businesslike. So why had he let his feelings grow?

He should have guarded his heart better and should have already learned his lesson about losing those he loved.

Never again.

Loving people led to hurt and heartache. That's all. He'd be better off with just himself and Boone. He didn't need a mother for his child. They'd gotten by already, and they'd get by again.

He straightened his shoulders and swallowed the pain crowding into his throat. Then he hardened his heart. "Let's go. I need to get my son back."

18

Genevieve read the final telegram from Papa's solicitor, Mr. Morgan.

With the rain tapping against the mercantile window, the lighting was dim and the words faint. But after spending the morning and part of the afternoon sitting in the mercantile and communicating with Mr. Morgan, she'd finally received exactly what she'd requested.

Mr. Morgan's telegram reassured her he'd located the best lawyer in Denver, who would arrive tomorrow to help Ryder fight to keep Boone. Of course, she hadn't revealed to Mr. Morgan that Ryder was her husband and Boone was now her stepchild. That information didn't matter at the moment.

All that truly mattered was finding a way to keep Sadie from taking away Boone.

Mr. Morgan had revealed that Lenora had already discovered Genevieve's whereabouts. Although Mr.

Morgan didn't have the ability to communicate the details via a telegram, Genevieve guessed that the news about the missing heiress in all the major newspapers across the country, as well as the offer of a reward, had brought forth plenty of information.

Although she'd already decided to tell Ryder the truth about her identity, she'd wanted to wait to share everything with him once the situation with Sadie was resolved. But now, according to Mr. Morgan, two bodyguards were already on their way to escort her back to New York City, which meant she'd have to tell Ryder everything sooner rather than later.

She hefted the sling in front of her, glad that Boone had finally fallen asleep. He'd been fussy since leaving the ranch yesterday after Sadie's threats.

She brushed a hand across his puckered forehead, wishing she could as easily smooth out the bumps he was sure to face in the coming weeks. Would he cry because he missed her? Would he wonder where she'd gone?

Now faced with the stark reality of having to leave Ryder and Boone, she wanted to find a way to make the situation work. Could she stay? Or maybe she could live part of the time in New York and part in Colorado?

With a sigh, she tucked the last telegram into her pocket along with the others from Mr. Morgan.

The store proprietor, a saggy cigar dangling from his mouth, stood abruptly from his place in front of the telegram machine. "Another one, ma'am."

Gray-haired and weathered, the proprietor had been attentive to her every need all day. After giving him forty dollars and promising him forty more if he was able to help her, he'd treated her like royalty. He'd sent the telegrams without any questions and had relayed the responses as soon as they'd come in. He'd found baby formula and a bottle for Boone. He'd located extra diapers. And he'd even made sure she'd had a noon meal and hot coffee delivered from Frisco's only eating establishment.

The hotel owner had been just as accommodating last night, reminding her more than ever just how much her wealth could buy her and how privileged she truly was. On some level she'd already known that, but her papa had always warned her about becoming arrogant and taught her to be generous, which was why she'd followed in his footsteps by remaining involved in so many charities.

However, after the past weeks of living simply and going without so many of the luxuries she was accustomed to, she was more sensitive than usual to the power she could wield. She supposed in some way she'd always taken her money and power for granted, and now she realized just how much she had, perhaps in a way she never had before.

Whatever the case, the store proprietor had been a

godsend. And now, after knowing that Ryder would have the best lawyer coming to defend him, she felt comfortable returning to the ranch with Boone. It was past time to go if she hoped to arrive before Ryder.

If he got home early, she didn't want him to worry where she was. After all, she hadn't left a note or any indication of where she'd gone. She'd considered sending Virgil, the livery owner, out to the ranch with word for Ross because she hadn't wanted him to worry either. But she hadn't wanted to take any chances that Sadie or Axe or the lawyer might be watching for her or even waiting in hiding.

The store owner bent his head and scanned the message. "This one is from . . . Lenora."

Lenora? A shiver of trepidation raced up Genevieve's spine.

She took the note and silently read the message written in the proprietor's neat penmanship: *If you return home at once, we will not prosecute Ryder Oakley for his crimes.*

Crimes? Ryder had done nothing wrong.

Yet, even though he hadn't, Lenora would figure out a way to accuse him of something, just as she had with Prescott and Mr. Price. Then he would be ruined. Even if he wasn't ruined, he would certainly have a much more difficult time being able to keep Boone, even with the best lawyer coming to his defense and proving what a good father he was.

No, she absolutely couldn't let Lenora hurt Ryder or Boone. But how could she protect them when Lenora had control over her now just as she always had? And she still wasn't strong enough or smart enough to break free.

"I am ready to leave now." She forced a smile for the store proprietor. "If you would ask Virgil to accompany me back to the ranch, I would appreciate that very much."

The store owner shifted his cigar to the opposite side of his mouth. "Of course, ma'am."

She paid him what she'd originally offered and then another twenty-dollar bill, knowing she wouldn't have need of the cash beyond a day or two, when the bodyguards would arrive for her. With only a few things in her room to collect, she started across the street to the town's only hotel, hunching over Boone to protect him from the rain.

All she could think about was that first day in Frisco when she'd stepped off the stagecoach and how free she'd felt. For once in her life, she'd done something alone, without servants, without drivers, without solicitors, and without her papa or Lenora. She'd made it to the West, and she'd been so proud of herself for her accomplishment.

But what had she really accomplished after all? She hadn't outsmarted Lenora. In fact, she'd only lasted a month before Lenora had tracked her down. And she'd only lasted a month of being independent and surviving on her own.

The truth was, she'd made a mess of things for Ryder by coming. She would confuse him and probably hurt him once she told him the truth about her identity—and she intended to do so just as soon as he returned home tonight. She'd also confuse poor little Boone once she was gone.

To make matters worse, she'd cause more rumors for Ryder over another failed marriage. Because ultimately, that's how the community would view the situation. They'd think she'd left him . . . the same way Sadie had left him.

"Oh dear," she whispered as she stepped around a puddle and leaped onto the lone wooden stair of the hotel. "I never meant for this to happen."

Of course she hadn't. She could almost hear Lenora's patronizing tone telling her that she was young and naïve and needed someone directing her so that she didn't get herself into trouble.

Genevieve pushed open the hotel door and hurried out of the rain. She swiped off her wet hat and brushed the loose strands of damp hair from her face, then froze as she took in the man sitting in a parlor that consisted of a few mismatched stuffed chairs and a round pedestal table off to one side, where men had been playing cards and drinking last night.

The fellow currently in the room was wearing a long coat, but he'd taken off his coonskin cap and braced it on his knee. His long brown hair was pulled back in a leather strap but was still messy. His brown eyes were already watching her, as if he'd seen her approach from the street.

"Tanner?"

He rose from his chair and nodded at her solemnly.

Her heart pumped an extra beat of anticipation in the hope of seeing Ryder somewhere, but another glance around the room didn't make him appear.

As she returned her gaze to Tanner and his grave expression, her heart stopped altogether. And suddenly she knew. This wasn't a pleasant social call. This was a serious meeting—one that wouldn't go well for her.

"I tracked you here." Tanner offered the explanation quietly, even as his gaze darted up the stairway toward the second floor.

"I see." But how and why?

She glanced out the window to the closest hitching post, and sure enough, Ryder's horse was tied up. In her haste to get out of the rain, she'd missed seeing it.

Tanner's eyes seemed to warn her. "Ryder's upstairs in your room waiting to speak with you."

Ryder had to be terribly angry with her for leaving without a word and forcing him to have to track her down.

She couldn't keep her shoulders from slumping as she reached the stairway railing.

"Wait."

She halted and cast Tanner a tentative look, wanting him to reassure her that everything would be all right.

But tension drew a line between his brows. "He wanted me to hold the baby for him."

Hold Boone? Why? She cradled the baby in the sling protectively for only a moment, then nodded. "Of course." It would be easier to have a conversation with Ryder if Boone wasn't distracting or interrupting them.

She slipped the sling over her shoulder and handed the baby to Tanner. Then she started up the steps, each one creaking loudly as if to announce her arrival.

There were only four private rooms, and she'd requested the largest of the four. Last night she hadn't been able to resist ordering a steaming hot bath in a large tub. It was the first she'd had like it since leaving home, and she'd soaked in the water for at least an hour while Boone napped.

Now, as she made her way down the hallway that had a worn runner muting her steps, her heart alternated between desire and dread. She couldn't deny that she'd missed Ryder, but she also had to disclose everything. And she loathed that in doing so, she would cause him more problems.

But hopefully, when she told him about the lawyer

who was coming as well as the housekeeper that she'd soon arrange for him, he wouldn't be as upset at her.

At the door, she hesitated. She combed back her damp hair, then plucked at her bodice, hoping it wasn't too revealing now that it was wet.

Finally, drawing in a breath, she swung the door open and stepped inside.

With his overpowering rugged brawn, Ryder stood in front of the window overlooking Main Street, staring out. Like Tanner, he'd probably seen her crossing from the mercantile a moment ago. If so, what was he thinking?

She closed the door and waited for him to turn, to level his angry eyes upon her the same way he had on Tanner that night at his family's when they'd fought.

He didn't turn. But the muscle in his neck flexed.

"I owe you an apology, Ryder."

"You do?" He spun, and sure enough the anger was there, blazing in his eyes. "For what?"

"For leaving and not letting anyone know where I went. I was trying to keep Boone safe, but I should have figured out a way to send word to Ross regarding my intentions."

Ryder wore an oiled cloak that hung open to reveal his usual denim trousers and flannel shirt underneath. His tan Stetson was wet, and the brim was drooping, but he kept it on, as though he wasn't planning on staying long.

"And what exactly are your intentions, Genevieve?"

He spoke her name with more emphasis than normal.

"I wanted to keep Sadie from finding Boone." She didn't care that her voice held a note of desperation—although she wasn't sure why she was feeling desperate, only that she knew something was wrong, and she wanted to make it right. "You have to believe me."

"And why should I believe anything you say?"

Her pulse slowed. Had he already figured out her identity? Was that why he was angry?

His gaze held hers for another long moment before he turned and stared out the window again. His back was stiff, his shoulders rigid, and his hands fisted.

Yes, he must have discovered who she really was. Maybe he'd seen a newspaper article. Or perhaps someone had told him. Maybe Tanner?

It didn't really matter how he'd found out. All that mattered was making him understand she hadn't meant for things to work out this way.

But what had she expected? To deceive him forever and get away with it?

She shook her head, loathing herself in this moment for her stupidity. Yes, she certainly had been as naïve as Lenora accused her of being, and possibly more so. She never should have made plans on her own, shouldn't have presumed she could be independent.

She crossed to him so that she was standing beside him. "I'm sorry, Ryder," she whispered. "So sorry."

His posture radiated his hurt—hurt she'd caused because of her deceitfulness and thoughtlessness and her callousness. She'd really only been thinking about her own situation when she'd made the plans, and she hadn't given enough consideration to what Ryder and Boone needed.

She waited for him to turn and tell her how awful she was, but he didn't move.

"Please talk to me."

His jaw flexed again.

Did he hate her now?

Heat spread through the backs of her eyes. "Please?"

Slowly, he turned until he was facing her. His expression was dark and stormy . . . but his eyes probed hers, pleading with her to give him some hope or a logical explanation for what she'd done.

But truly, she'd been selfish and had taken the easy way out of her difficulties by fleeing instead of staying and learning to be strong in the face of Lenora's control. There was no excuse for her selfishness and no way she could explain it away.

At her silence, his eyes began to narrow.

"Wait." She lifted both hands and cupped his cheeks.

He didn't speak, but at least he didn't attempt to break the contact.

"I love you, Ryder." The words spilled out before she could stop them. But once spoken, she knew it was the truth and the only thing she could say.

19

She loved him?

She couldn't mean it, could she? Was she just saying the words to soothe him? To make his anger go away?

He knew he ought to contradict her. But at the trembling of her fingers against his cheeks and the vulnerability widening her eyes, all the anger that had festered inside him since Worth's General Store dissipated, and he couldn't make himself deny her love.

Yes, he still needed so many more answers. He needed to understand what had driven her to such deception— why she'd resorted to answering a newspaper advertisement, and why she'd fled west and used a different name.

After having gotten to know just how kind and caring she was, there had to be a reason for everything she'd done. Maybe she'd been in trouble. Maybe she still was. And maybe he could protect her.

At the moment, however, her declaration of love continued to swell within him. Was it true?

He needed to hear her say it again.

"What did you say?" he whispered, unable to stop himself from taking in every part of her face—her smooth forehead, arched eyebrows, long lashes, high cheekbones, perfect lips, gently pointed chin. Her skin was paler than usual, making her eyes bluer.

How could she be more beautiful today than yesterday? How was that possible? And why did he have to be so attracted to her?

He didn't want to need her, but after being away from her since yesterday, he was famished for her. And after the past hours of not knowing where she was or what had happened, his relief at finding her only added fuel to the need that was combusting inside him.

"I'm sorry," she whispered again.

"No, after that." He knew he shouldn't let his gaze drop to her damp bodice, but he did anyway. And through the wet material, he could make out the lacy outline of her chemise.

"I love you." This time as she spoke the words, she lifted on her toes, as though she wanted to offer him a kiss.

She loved him. She'd said it twice, which meant she hadn't spoken it accidentally. And she wanted to kiss him.

What more did he need? They could work out all the

rest in time, couldn't they?

Maybe he was too easily giving way to his desires and wasn't thinking logically about the situation, but suddenly, all that mattered was kissing her.

He dipped down and met her, covering her mouth with his. The moment of their meshing, his body trembled with a wanting that went so deep it threatened to undo him. All he knew was that he'd been waiting for a long time to have a love like this, and he'd finally found it. Maybe not in the way he'd been expecting, but it was still there in all the messiness and beauty mixed together.

Now, as their lips heated against one another, their kissing felt like one of the volcanoes he'd read about in ancient history—one that had lain dormant but was now bubbling to life, burning hot and flaming explosively, ready to burn everything in its path.

Her hands slid upward from his cheeks to his hat. In the next instant, she lifted it from his head, tossed it on the bed, and then dove her fingers into his hair, all while meeting his kiss stroke for stroke.

At her grip tightening within his hair, he couldn't hold back a groan. His hands skimmed up her back and at the same time drew her closer so that the distance closed between them, and in the next instant she and all her beautiful curves were pressed tightly against him.

There was no more keeping the heat of their passion dormant. No more denying it was there. No more pretending it didn't exist. They couldn't. Not after this kiss.

In fact, he was burning up with such fervor that he had half a mind to scoop her up, lie down on the bed with her, and let them get carried away. But he couldn't—not with Tanner waiting with Boone downstairs.

He had to rein in his passion for now. They'd have plenty of time later to get carried away. Shoot, they'd have every day for the rest of their lives to kiss as long and as often as they wanted.

With a self-control that made his hands tremble, he gentled the kiss, slowing it, letting the exploration of each other's mouths grow more languid. But even as he did so, the passion was taut within him, the need for her strong, so that he wanted to do more than just explore her mouth.

Bracing his shoulders, he broke the kiss. Then he braced his hands on her shoulders, trying to make himself step back. But even as he did so, he bent in and stole another kiss.

She released a soft sound of pleasure the moment his lips connected again, and she swayed close.

"I love you too." His declaration was hoarse against her lips, and he wanted to wrap her up again into his arms and hold her and never let her go.

But at the echo of his words, she halted and stiffened.

She released her hold of his hair and dropped her arms to her sides.

He couldn't let go of her, though. He rubbed his hands from her shoulders, down her arms, and then to her hips. He loved feeling every soft part of her and couldn't get enough. How had he lived without this touching?

She took another step back and then another, breaking their contact. She didn't stop until she was pressed against the wall. "I'm sorry, Ryder. I'm so sorry." Even in the low light of the cloudy afternoon, he could see the tears pooling in her eyes.

She'd already apologized once. Why was she doing so again? "We'll work it all out, darlin'," he said softly. But even as he tried to reassure her, a low tremor of anxiety began to pulse through him. Something wasn't right.

"I never meant to fall in love with you." Her voice wobbled. "I have no right to love you. Not when I have to return to New York City."

"You don't have to—"

"I have no choice. My stepmother is my guardian, and she's sent men to retrieve me."

His mind was tumbling in an effort to understand everything she was saying. "So you came to escape her?"

She nodded. "Constance was a friend of mine who worked at the orphanage. She had two marriage proposals, and so we decided I would take yours. And since you just wanted a mother for your baby, I didn't think it would matter if I came and took care of the baby for a while."

"For a while?"

"Until I turn twenty-one next summer and am no longer under my stepmother's authority."

His mind reeled with her revelation. "So you never planned to stay?" He couldn't keep his tone from turning hard.

"No." She was breathing heavily from their kissing, her chest still rising and falling rapidly. Her lips were swollen, and her cheeks contained a pale pink. And even though he was trying to absorb the information she was finally sharing, his body tightened with the need to crush her against him, kiss her hard, and make her promise to stay with him forever.

But it was finally time for him to know the truth about everything, and he couldn't let his need for her blind him any longer.

"What were you going to do?" he asked. "Use me and Boone for a year, then throw us away when you no longer needed us?"

She released a small cry of despair. "That's not fair. I would never do that."

"Then what?" An ache stabbed his chest, like a knife plunged deep. "How were you planning to tell me you were going? And how were you expecting Boone to handle losing his ma?"

"I thought I could take care of him like I did the orphans, loving him and yet not getting too close."

"Is that right?" The anger from earlier was returning, but this time laced with pain. "And I suppose you were hoping he wouldn't get close to you either?"

A tear slipped out and trailed down her cheek. "I admit, I did not anticipate that we'd both grow so attached to each other so soon."

"So after a year, you were hoping he wouldn't need a ma any longer?"

"No, I'd planned to hire a housekeeper or nursemaid as a replacement."

"Really? Did you think your plan would work?"

She paused. Her face crumpled, and she placed both hands over her face. "No. Of course not. It was a terrible idea. I understand that now."

He knew he was being hard on her. Because he'd initially considered hiring help for Boone too. But somewhere along the way, he'd realized Boone needed a permanent woman in his life. And he'd also realized he needed a permanent woman too.

Genevieve sniffled behind her hands. "I never should have agreed to take Constance's place. But you mentioned that you just wanted a partnership. Just a mother. Not a wife."

Just a mother. Not a wife. Maybe he hadn't said those

exact words in his communication with Constance, but that's what he'd thought he'd wanted.

She dropped her hands to reveal her tear-stained cheeks. "I thought I could do what you asked—take care of the baby in exchange for a place to live. But I was wrong."

And he'd been wrong too. "I thought all I wanted was a partnership. And maybe with any other woman, I would have been satisfied with that." He blew out a tense breath. "But not with you."

"You didn't want a wife, Ryder."

"I do now." His voice came out harsh.

She was studying his face, as though she was preparing herself for a goodbye. "I can't be your wife."

"You already are."

She shook her head, the tears dripping down her cheeks again. "If I don't leave you and return to New York City, my stepmother will find a way to destroy you."

"I'd like to see her try." He started toward her, the anger inside evaporating and leaving behind desperation.

She held out a hand to stop his progression. "She's already trumped up charges against you."

"Like what?" He halted only a few steps from her.

"I don't know. But she'll find a way to slander you, accuse you of crimes, and ruin you as a way to punish me. And right now, you need your reputation to stay unblemished so that you can win the fight against Sadie to keep Boone."

He paused his thoughts and let her warning sink in. As much as he wanted to protest that he didn't care what her stepmother did to him, he didn't just have himself to think about. He had to do what was right for Boone now, too, and couldn't jeopardize his parental rights.

Genevieve swiped at her cheeks. "Lenora has already destroyed the life and reputation of one good man that I'd intended to marry. I won't let her destroy your life now too."

Had Genevieve been engaged to someone else? And if so, how recently?

Although a flicker of jealousy flared to life inside him, something else did too—the realization that he knew so little about this woman. In fact, everything he'd thought he'd known was based on a lie.

Instead of being a poor working-class woman, she was wealthy and had a lifestyle that he knew nothing about— one so far removed from the wilderness of Colorado that it was unfathomable to him. She had probably intended to marry someone wealthy, within the same social circles and with an exemplary family history. Not an orphan with no idea who his family was or where they'd come from.

In fact, he couldn't fault her stepmother for being opposed to Genevieve running away across the country and marrying a stranger. If Genevieve had been his family, he would have been against her doing that too.

"I love you, Ryder," she whispered, her eyes brimming with anguish. "And as hard as it will be to leave you and Boone, I have to do it. There is no other way to keep you both together and safe."

She watched him expectantly, as though hoping he'd offer another solution, a way for them to be together in spite of all the obstacles.

But she'd been born to have the kind of life he could never provide for her on his little homestead in the mountains. If Sadie, who'd grown up in the high country, couldn't adjust to life on the ranch, how would Genevieve make it? She would grow restless—if she wasn't already. Eventually she might become resentful of having so little and being so far away from the life she'd always known.

Even if they'd never had her stepmother to worry about, Genevieve didn't belong here. She deserved a man who could give her everything she was used to, not a broken man with a broken past who'd never planned for a future.

Yes, she'd said she loved him, and he most definitely loved her, but maybe love wasn't always enough.

He steeled his shoulders, knowing what he needed to do. She was leaving him because she cared about him. And he was doing the same for her. There was no sense in dragging out the goodbye.

He gave her a nod. Then he swiped his hat from the

bed, jammed it on his head, and crossed to the door. He didn't pause as he opened the door and stepped into the hallway. He didn't pause when he shut the door and started away from the room. And he didn't pause even when a muted sob came from behind the closed door.

His chest burned and his throat ached, but he forced himself to take one step after another. If he didn't, he knew he'd never be able to leave her behind, and he'd destroy them both.

20

Could she really ride away from Summit County?

Genevieve's heart pounded a hard protest as the stagecoach from Denver drew nearer, rumbling down Frisco's main thoroughfare and slowing as it neared the livery.

"I can't do this." She took a step back but bumped into Emmett, one of the bodyguards Lenora had sent to accompany her to New York City.

The older of the two, Emmett had a gravity about him that told her he took his job to protect her seriously. His arms were crossed, and his black suit coat pulled taut across his thick arms and shoulders. With his bowler pulled low and his revolvers holstered at his waist in full sight of everyone, he certainly had an intimidating aura.

For as daunting as Emmett was, however, he'd been polite, even tender with her during all their interactions since his arrival two days ago, shortly after Ryder had left her alone in the hotel room.

Her throat still ached every time she replayed Ryder's walking away. His footsteps had taken him down the stairs and out the door, and she hadn't been able to resist rushing to the window and watching him mount and ride away with Boone and Tanner, hoping he'd look back so that she could see his face one last time.

But with his head down and his shoulders slumped, he hadn't so much as peeked her way. When he'd disappeared from sight, she'd thrown herself onto the bed and sobbed until there hadn't been any more tears left.

Even though she'd tried not to hope, she'd hoped anyway that he would ride back into town and tell her that she couldn't leave, that he wanted her more than anything, and that they'd find a way to keep out of Lenora's clutches.

Maybe they could run away together? Someplace farther west? Perhaps to Canada?

But as Genevieve tried to plot a safe place where Lenora wouldn't be able to find them, she realized the effort was hopeless. The offer of a reward always paid off. It was just one more way that having an endless supply of money worked to one's advantage.

Besides, she could never ask Ryder to leave his ranch—not after he'd labored so hard over the past months to build it up and make it what it was. He loved it—loved the land, loved the work, and loved the wildness of it all.

Even if he could start over someplace new, the Oakleys meant everything to him, and he wouldn't want to part ways with his adopted family. He most certainly wouldn't want to leave Tanner behind. Although she hadn't thought to ask how Ryder's meeting with Tanner had gone, the fact that Tanner had helped him likely meant he'd begun to repair their relationship again.

"You've got to do this, Mrs. Oakley." Emmett didn't budge from his spot behind her. "Mrs. Hollis won't have it any other way."

Genevieve understood full well what he wasn't saying aloud—that if she didn't come with him and his companion, Lenora would just send other men, who might not be as cordial and accommodating. And she could give Emmett credit for using her married name, even though, apparently, Lenora had instructed the bodyguards not to.

As the stagecoach driver reined the teams of horses to a halt, Genevieve braced herself for what she knew she had to do. She had to go.

Although the rain had moved off, the ground was still muddy, and the horses and the stagecoach were caked in mire and in much need of a washing. But that wouldn't happen today. Not when arrangements had been made for the stagecoach not to continue to the next stop on the line. Instead, it was to turn around and drive her directly to the train station in Denver.

Regardless, there was still time for Ryder to reach town and stop her before she boarded.

Her gaze strayed to the path that led south of Frisco to Ryder's ranch. The rocky trail was as deserted now as it had been every other time she'd looked today and yesterday. Ryder wasn't coming after her.

Why couldn't she just accept the reality of the situation? In her heart she knew that he and Boone would be safer without a connection to her, without any way for Lenora to hurt them. But that didn't prevent her body from aching with a need for them both that wouldn't go away.

She couldn't stop thinking about the kiss Ryder had given her in the hotel room. That moment with him had only solidified how much she loved him. She wasn't sure when the love had developed—maybe slowly over the past weeks. But in the face of losing him, she'd known that she loved him more than anything else. The emotions had tumbled through her, picking up speed and snowballing until the weight and depth of the love had been crushing and powerful.

He'd said he loved her too. And from the passionate way he'd responded and the way he'd looked at her—as though she were the only thing that mattered in life— she'd known he meant the declaration.

Yet he'd still walked out of her life, and he'd made no

effort to walk back into it. Maybe she needed to be the one to go after him.

As before, a hundred questions took flight in her head. What was she doing? Why was she leaving the man she loved? Why couldn't she simply ride back to the ranch and tell him she wanted to go on with life the way it had been over the past month? Why did anything have to change at all?

Rationally, she knew the answer to each of her questions. And rationally, she knew that because she loved him so much, she would get on the stagecoach and ride away.

But what if the goodbye didn't have to be forever? What if he would be willing to wait for her to turn twenty-one and gain control over her life?

Even as she allowed the hope for the future to spark to life, she rapidly snuffed it out. It wasn't fair to ask Ryder to wait a year to give Boone a mother. Most likely he'd place another advertisement in the newspapers and find someone else who wanted the life he was offering. Although that prospect sent despair through her, she truly did want the best for both him and Boone.

In the meantime, what would happen to their marriage? Would they have to file for a divorce? She wasn't sure how that worked but guessed Lenora and Mr. Morgan would have a say in what happened next.

The stagecoach door opened, and a well-dressed

young gentleman with a neatly trimmed mustache poked his head out. Wearing a fashionable black top hat, frock coat, and day suit, he was certainly out of place compared to most of the plainly dressed men who lived in the high country.

He scanned the town with his keen, bright eyes before letting his gaze come to rest upon her. He took her in from her straw hat to her mud-splattered skirt. If he was shocked by her appearance, he didn't show it, and instead offered her a wide smile. "Miss Hollis, I presume?"

She was Mrs. Oakley. But she suspected most people outside of Summit County wouldn't have learned of her marriage—at least, not yet. "Yes, I am she, but I am now married and go by Mrs. Oakley."

"I'm Mr. Andridge, the lawyer you requested."

She studied him again, this time taking in his youthful face. He looked her age, or perhaps a year or two older. Much too young to be a lawyer, especially the experienced one she needed.

She held back a frustrated sigh. She'd telegrammed Mr. Morgan to make arrangements to send the *very best* lawyer. Not the *youngest*. What had happened? Had he misunderstood her communication? Had the telegram operator written it down wrong?

When she arrived in Denver, she would insist on stopping at the best law firm in the city, and she would make arrangements for another lawyer to ride up to the high country. This time, preferably an older gentleman with experience who would be able to help Ryder. Not this young fellow.

Mr. Andridge stepped down from the stagecoach, brandishing a silver walking stick. Gingerly he made his way through the mud toward her and then bowed with a flourish, removing his hat and revealing fair hair. "Pleased to meet you, Mrs. Oakley."

She couldn't say the same of him. Nevertheless, she gave him a polite smile. "Mr. Andridge, thank you for coming. But I think there's been a mistake."

He straightened, but one of his legs had an odd bend to it. "And what mistake might that be?"

She hesitated, not wanting to discourage him if he already had his heart set on helping her. But she needed the right man for the job. Providing an expert lawyer who could help Ryder keep Boone was vitally important to her, more so than anything else at the moment. "I was expecting someone older and with more experience. In fact, I requested the very best lawyer in all of Denver."

"I see." The cheerfulness in his expression didn't wane. Instead, his keen eyes appraised first Emmett and then the other bodyguard, who was just inside the livery, waiting beside her luggage.

"I'm sorry for wasting your time in coming all this way."

"Yes, it's clear that whoever made the arrangements

doesn't have your interests at heart."

"Or it's possible the telegram was decoded incorrectly."

Mr. Andridge pulled a telegram from his inner coat pocket and held it out to her. "Mr. Morgan requested the newest lawyer in our firm."

"That cannot be correct." She took the card and scanned to indeed find those very words, including the rest of the statement about how the matter wasn't urgent, even though she'd made clear that it was.

"Since I am the only lawyer in my newly opened office, I decided that I would have to avail myself."

She'd always assumed Papa's lawyer cared about her well-being. But if he did, why hadn't he helped her with her very specific request? If the telegram and Mr. Andridge could be trusted, then it appeared as though Mr. Morgan had done the opposite of what she'd wanted.

Was Mr. Andridge correct in his statement that her long-time lawyer didn't have her interests at heart?

She shook her head. Mr. Morgan had been with the family for years, and her papa had trusted him. There had to be some other explanation for the mix-up.

Mr. Andridge's eyes held only sincerity and kindness. "Although I am busier than you might imagine for one as *young* and *inexperienced* as myself, I concluded that a woman running away from her fortune must be in need of an unbiased advocate with nothing to gain. And if not an advocate, then at the very least a friend."

Was he right? Did she need an unbiased advocate with nothing to gain? She shook her head. "I am not the one in need of a lawyer, Mr. Andridge—"

"Perhaps you are in more need of one than you realize."

Maybe she was. And maybe when she got back to New York City she would have to seek out new legal counsel, if she could find a way to do so without Lenora being any the wiser.

"Right now I need a lawyer for my . . . husband."

Once again, if Mr. Andridge was surprised, he didn't show it. And she liked that quality about him. Instead, he nodded and waved his cane toward the hotel behind her. "I wonder if we could find somewhere more private to speak about the matter."

If this young man had been insightful enough to see all that he had about her in such a short time, then surely she could take a moment to explain the threats against Ryder and garner his perspective on the matter.

Emmett glared at the young lawyer. "She needs to go."

Mr. Andridge waved his cane at the conveyance. "I'm sure waiting five more minutes won't pose a problem. The stagecoach driver will need at least that before he's ready for the return drive."

Emmett's scowl didn't relent, but he nodded his head.

"Fine. Five minutes."

Several minutes later, Genevieve was perched in one of the mismatched chairs in the hotel's parlor with Mr. Andridge across from her while she finished explaining Ryder's predicament with Sadie and Boone.

Mr. Andridge rested his hand on his silver walking stick, at the ready beside his chair. "It sounds as though you care about both Ryder and Boone."

Care was inadequate to describe her feelings, but she nodded anyway. "I do believe Sadie deserves a chance to be involved in Boone's life, and I hope for Boone's sake she will make an effort to love him and get to know him. But . . ."

"But she doesn't care about him yet and only wants the child so that she can keep a measure of control over Ryder."

"Yes." How had the young lawyer deduced the truth so quickly? "Do you think you'll be able to find a way for Ryder to keep Boone?"

"Since she gave up the child at birth and Ryder has already proven to be the more responsible parent, most judges will recognize his efforts."

"But her lawyer brought up the Tender Years Doctrine."

"Such a philosophy is gaining eminence, but paternal custody is still the primary preference."

Genevieve could feel the tension easing from her

shoulders. Mr. Andridge seemed knowledgeable enough. Perhaps he would be able to fight for Ryder after all.

"If things go the way I predict," Mr. Andridge continued, "I suspect I won't need more than one meeting with her before she drops the case."

"You do exude confidence, Mr. Andridge."

"Then you'd like me to handle the case, even though I am young and inexperienced?" His question was accompanied by a smile—one that said he was teasing her.

She smiled in return. "Yes. And if you succeed in winning the case, I will pay you double what you normally charge."

"No need. I will only accept what is fair."

Her esteem for this lawyer was growing with every passing moment. "Thank you, Mr. Andridge." She could only hope his confidence and clear savvy would help him and that he truly would succeed.

Mr. Andridge was silent for several beats, so that bits of conversation between the stagecoach driver and Virgil carried through the slightly open window—mostly talk about the coming colder weather and the snow that would close the mountain passes in the next month or two, putting an end to the stagecoach travel.

If only she'd been able to hide for another month, until the first big snowfall. Maybe then she would have been stranded in the high country until spring, with no chance of Lenora tracking her down.

She expelled a breath.

Mr. Andridge's sharp gaze homed in on her face. "When you're able to return to Colorado and your husband, I assure you the matter will be settled."

She could see what he was doing. He was pushing her for more information about her situation with Ryder. She had no reason not to tell him the truth about her marriage, especially since it might have a bearing on the outcome of Boone's custody. "It is unlikely I will be returning, Mr. Andridge. You should know that my stepmother is my guardian until I turn twenty-one, and she will require me to dissolve the marriage." Although the telegram hadn't been that specific, Genevieve knew that was what Lenora would want.

"I see."

"Will the failed marriage have an impact on Ryder being able to keep Boone?"

"I do not believe it will."

She prayed it wouldn't.

At Emmett's stepping into the doorway and motioning that it was time to go, she stood. "Will you send me a telegram as soon as the matter is settled?"

"Of course." Mr. Andridge rose to his feet and situated his silver cane in front of himself, his gaze never once leaving her face. "I've only just met you, but it is easy to see that you are a strong woman."

A scoffing sound pushed for release, but she bit it back. "I believe you are mistaken."

"You came here, didn't you?"

"Yes, but—"

"If you broke free once, I suspect you can find the strength to do it again."

His words stirred something inside her, but before she could find the words to respond, Emmett began crossing to her, his expression severe upon Mr. Andridge. Although she wanted to continue her discussion with the young lawyer, she knew she would have to be satisfied for today.

As though realizing the same, Mr. Andridge bowed his head. "My original offer stands. I am your humble servant if you ever need me again."

With a final nod of thanks, she allowed Emmett to lead her from the parlor, out the door, and to the waiting stagecoach, where the other bodyguard had already taken a seat beside the driver.

Within minutes, she was settled against the bench with Emmett in the spot across from her. She peered out the window at Mr. Andridge, who now stood in the doorway of the hotel, leaning on his cane.

His words rolled through her like the wheels of the conveyance beneath her, bumping and jostling and unsettling her. *"If you broke free once, I suspect you can find the strength to do it again."*

If only he knew the truth. She'd proven she didn't have the strength. She was returning home as a failure. And in the process, she was losing the man who'd come to mean more to her than all the riches in the world.

21

Ryder was dying inside a little more each day that he was apart from Genevieve.

He paced near the door in Mr. Irving's office, juggling Boone in the sling. The baby was fussier than usual, probably missing Genevieve too—or at least sensing his distress that Genevieve was gone.

He bounced Boone and tried to focus on what Mr. Irving was saying, but he couldn't think of anything except the fact that Genevieve had left Colorado yesterday.

Mr. Andridge sat beside Sadie, both of them across from Mr. Irving at his desk, which was meticulous without a single pen or piece of paper out of place. The whole office was organized neatly—the shelves of books in alphabetical order and rows of files cataloged to perfection.

Mr. Andridge waved a hand at Sadie. "Why don't you

allow the baby's mother to have a turn calming him?"

The question broke through Ryder's despair. He paused and faced the lawyer who'd shown up on his ranch yesterday afternoon with the news that Genevieve had hired him to defend his rights to have Boone.

Ryder had told Mr. Andridge he didn't want to be beholden to Genevieve and that he'd figure things out on his own. But when the young lawyer had stated the reasonable fee he was charging Genevieve, Ryder had decided it was low enough that he would pay it himself.

Mr. Andridge had arranged the meeting with Mr. Irving and Sadie for this morning. Sadie had been the first to talk and had already explained how terrible the pregnancy and birthing had been and how that had influenced her into giving up Boone. She'd been in tears while sharing the difficulty of the past summer with missing Boone and realizing she wanted to be the baby's mother after all.

Mr. Irving sat rigidly at his desk across from them, his slender face serious. He combed his fingers through his long sideburns and bushy beard, his gaze now upon Sadie as he waited for her to agree to hold Boone.

Mr. Andridge was much younger than Breckenridge's only lawyer. Even so, Ryder had been impressed so far with the fellow's intelligence and depth of understanding of the laws. Now he was also watching Sadie but was leaning back in his chair, one leg crossed over the other, holding a silver cane.

He twisted his hand on the curve of the cane and now shifted his gaze to Ryder. "If Sadie wishes to take over, then it is important for her to get accustomed to caring for the infant."

Ryder's grip on Boone tightened, and he wanted to shake his head. Sadie had never held the baby, not even after he was born—had apparently claimed she was too exhausted. What would happen if she held Boone now? All it had taken was holding Boone once for him to fall in love with the little guy. Would it be the same for Sadie?

"Go on." Mr. Andridge's words were casual, but something in his expression was intense.

When they'd talked outside Mr. Irving's office a short while ago before the meeting, Mr. Andridge had encouraged him to trust him and follow his instructions. And now, even though Ryder didn't want to give Sadie a turn holding Boone, he knew he had no other option.

Ryder peered down at Boone. With his face scrunched and red, the boy released another wail—one containing his dissatisfaction with life. Or maybe the cry echoed Ryder's dissatisfaction with life. Because his whole life seemed turned upside down since he'd left Genevieve behind in the hotel room. Nothing made sense. Nothing else mattered. Nothing could end the turmoil inside.

"Ryder hasn't let me hold the baby." Sadie spoke with an edge of bitterness, as if she really was bothered by his overprotectiveness of Boone.

If Sadie was sincere about wanting a part in Boone's life, then he needed to give her the opportunity, didn't he? He needed to give Boone the opportunity too. The boy deserved to know his mother. Especially because Ryder already knew what it was like to be without a mother and had felt the emptiness inside for so many years.

Without giving himself the chance to change his mind, he crossed to where Sadie sat. But even as he stood in front of her and tried to lower Boone toward her, fear surged through him, and he couldn't make his muscles move.

Why did losses always seem to hit him the most? What was wrong with him that he couldn't keep the people he loved from leaving him? Was he such a failure that he couldn't make anyone happy enough to stay?

The swell of fear rose into his throat, just as it had over the past few days since Genevieve's leaving.

Mr. Andridge bumped him with his cane, forcing Ryder to look at him. "I'll tell you the same thing I told Genevieve. Not only am I your advocate but I'll also be your friend. That means whatever the outcome, you will never have to face your trials alone."

The sincerity in the man's eyes steadied Ryder and reminded him that even though there had been times in his life when he'd felt alone, ultimately, someone had always come along at just the right moment to help him. Those two cowboys who had taken the time to deliver him and Tanner to the orphanage. Kind orphanage workers over the years. Ma and Pa Oakley making them a part of the family. His siblings helping him time and time again over the past six months.

He'd had friends there to hold him up through it all. And maybe Providence had been there too, working behind the scenes in ways he hadn't realized.

Whatever the case, this young lawyer was here today, by his side. Mr. Andridge was right. No matter what the outcome might be, he wasn't alone.

Boone released another wail, this one louder than the last.

At Mr. Andridge's nod, Ryder extended the baby to Sadie. Yes, there was still the chance he could lose his son. But he wouldn't have to face the loss alone. And maybe with the help from all those who cared about him, he could fight to win Boone back. Was it possible he could fight to win Genevieve too?

The prospect sent life pumping back into his blood. He didn't know how he could overcome all the barriers that stood between them and get her back in his life, but after the past few days of feeling as though he was dead without her, he knew without a doubt he'd never loved anyone the way he did her. He needed her in his life.

With widening eyes, Sadie tentatively touched Boone.

"It's not fair that you want me to try to calm him down."

"It's all right." Ryder lowered the baby into her arms. "The first time I held him, he cried for hours straight. I thought something was wrong."

Sadie sat frozen in place, staring down at Boone as though he were a wailing wolf pup who might lunge at her.

"You can try bouncing him a little," he offered. "Maybe talk to him?"

She hesitated, then gave one bounce as she peered down at Boone's face. "Hey there."

Boone stopped crying and stared up at her.

Ryder's heart gave a hard thud. Did the boy already recognize Sadie as his mother?

"That's right." She held herself and the baby stiffly, as if one wrong move would cause him to start wailing again. "We'll get along just fine." She shot Ryder an I-told-you-so look.

"As I said"—Mr. Irving broke into the conversation as he watched Sadie—"I propose that you both get time with the baby."

Ryder had opposed Mr. Irving's suggestion from the start of their meeting, but now that Sadie was holding Boone, a knot formed in Ryder's chest. If Sadie wanted to be in Boone's life, he couldn't take that away from her. And although giving Boone over to her for periods of time wouldn't be ideal, it seemed only fair.

Mr. Andridge raised his brow at Ryder, as though to ask him if he was still opposed to the idea.

"Okay," Ryder said, although hesitantly. "I'm agreeable to both Sadie and me getting to spend time with Boone."

"I am agreeable too." Mr. Andridge brushed a speck off his light-gray suit trousers and didn't meet anyone's gaze. "Especially because that will ease Ryder's responsibilities since he is a single father again."

Sadie sat forward. "Single father?"

Mr. Andridge finally glanced up a little too innocently. "Yes, you didn't hear? Ryder's wife left for New York City yesterday."

Sadie shook her head. "No. I heard she was that runaway heiress but didn't know she was going back."

Boone let out a wail, one that startled Sadie so that she fumbled with the baby.

Ryder put out a steadying hand. "Careful now."

Sadie stood abruptly and thrust Boone back at him, giving him no choice but to take the crying baby.

Ryder cradled the infant against his shoulder and began to bounce him.

Sadie took a step toward the door. "If that woman is gone, then I don't need to be involved."

Even with Boone's wails filling the office, a strange silence filled Ryder, and he scowled. What was Sadie up to?

"What?" She shrugged. "I didn't know the woman. She was a stranger, and there was no telling if she would've made a good ma to Boone."

"She already was a good ma." Ryder couldn't keep his tone from filling with rapidly mounting anger.

Mr. Andridge was standing now too. "So what are you saying, Sadie? That you would like to make sure Ryder chooses a suitable mother, but that you do not want to be the mother yourself?"

"That about sums it up."

Mr. Irving released an exasperated breath.

Ryder's anger quickly faded as Mr. Andridge's tactic took shape. He'd made sure Ryder was agreeable and rational so that no one could find fault with him. Then he'd gotten Sadie to confess that she didn't really want the baby.

Ryder doubted she'd been pursuing having Boone because she wanted to make sure Genevieve was a suitable ma. She was just giving a convenient excuse. No, she'd likely felt threatened in some way by Genevieve's presence. Now that the threat was gone, she no longer needed to make herself appear to be better and worthier than the new woman in his life.

Sadie lifted her chin as if she was justified in her position. "If he's going to have another woman around my son, I ought to be able to help decide if she's fit."

"And what makes another woman fit to be a mother to Boone?"

"I don't know."

"I'd like to make a record of it." Mr. Andridge pulled out a piece of paper and unfolded it. "Then, if my client does want a caregiver or wife at some point again, we'll have a standard that he must abide by. Is that all right with you, Mr. Irving?"

"It sounds reasonable." Mr. Irving's expression contained a haggardness that indicated Sadie hadn't been particularly easy to defend.

"Good. Then how about I jot those qualities right here on this paper." Mr. Andridge took a pen from Mr. Irving's desk. "Tell us the most important qualities in the woman who will eventually become Boone's mother."

Sadie shrugged. "Well, she can't be yelling or hitting him."

Mr. Andridge's pen was poised above the paper. "So she must be kindhearted and loving?"

"Reckon that sounds right."

Mr. Andridge scribbled the words on the sheet. "Anything else?"

"Not that I can think of." Sadie was already making her way to the door.

"Then before you go, you will need to sign this paper saying that you're relinquishing your right to Boone—of course, with the stipulation that Ryder's wife will be kindhearted and loving toward Boone. If the wife is not, then you will have the right to fight Ryder again for custody."

Sadie looked at the sheet that Mr. Andridge was holding out and hesitated.

Ryder couldn't breathe past the anticipation now rising in his chest. Clearly the young lawyer had come prepared with the relinquishment agreement written up and had expected Sadie to sign over her rights.

Mr. Andridge was good. In fact, he was more than good. Not only was he a decent fellow, but he was shrewd and had guided the entire interaction the way he'd planned.

Mr. Irving stood. "I should read through the relinquishment first and make sure the terms are agreeable."

Sadie blew out an exasperated breath. "They're agreeable to me, Mr. Irving. Listening to the baby cry for a few minutes is enough for me to know that I don't want to have to listen to it any longer."

Within minutes, the document was signed, and Sadie was gone. Ryder stepped out of the lawyer's office with Mr. Andridge following behind and leaning on his cane. The side street wasn't as busy as the main thoroughfare, with only one other person walking out of a newly built boarding house across the street.

Boone was chewing on one of Ryder's fingers, and the

fussing had diminished—at least for the time being. Even though the sun was out, the wind blowing in from the north held a chilly bite for September.

"Thank you, Mr. Andridge. You were brilliant." Ryder stuck out his hand.

The lawyer shook it firmly. "I am grateful Genevieve gave me a chance to take the case. Most people assume that because I have a twisted leg, my mind doesn't work well either."

"Didn't assume that at all." Ryder couldn't keep from glancing down at Mr. Andridge's legs. There was something odd about the angle of his leg, but the fellow had obviously learned to compensate for the issue so that it was hardly noticeable.

"I would appreciate you relaying my thanks to Genevieve." Mr. Andridge leaned onto his cane.

"I'm afraid I won't be able to do that—"

"And when you see her, let her know that since she is married, her stepmother's guardianship is no longer binding."

The same anticipation as before gripped Ryder's chest.

"I have a friend from law school who works in New York City. I telegrammed him yesterday to do some investigating for me. Turns out, he was able to find information on the Hollis guardianship case."

Ryder didn't know much about Genevieve's

stepmother and all that had transpired, since she'd only shared a little in the hotel room in Frisco. But it had been clear the relationship was complicated. "So she's free to live without her stepmother?"

"The marriage supersedes the guardianship. She still cannot have access to her fortune until she turns twenty-one, but the stepmother no longer has legal power over her."

Ryder's mind began to race in a hundred different directions all at once. What did this mean? And what was his part in it? As her husband, did he have the power to help her finally be free the way she'd wanted?

Mr. Andridge's brow furrowed above his kind eyes. "I am afraid her trust in her lawyer has been misplaced."

Of course a woman as wealthy as Genevieve would have a lawyer directing her affairs. "You think he's been dishonest with her?"

"He's manipulating her. That was obvious from his telegram even before I rode up to Frisco."

If Genevieve was being controlled and manipulated, then it was no wonder she'd had no option but to run away and hide. Even though Ryder didn't like how Genevieve had deceived him, wishing she had been honest from the start, he could easily forgive her—had already forgiven her.

"What's in it for the lawyer?" Ryder's gut churned just thinking about anyone taking advantage of Genevieve, especially with how sweet and kind she was.

"If her lawyer is colluding with the stepmother, perhaps he has discovered a way they can gain access to part of her fortune."

"Then they're stealing from her?"

"I admit, it's pure conjecture on my part. But I cannot think of any other reason why the stepmother would be so anxious to have her return except to resume her guardianship."

Boone was now sucking on his own fist and making grunting noises.

An older fellow stepped out of the saloon next to Mr. Irving's office. He tipped his hat at the two of them before meandering down the street toward the main thoroughfare.

As soon as the man was out of hearing range, Mr. Andridge glanced around as if to make sure they were alone, then he spoke in a low voice. "Since marriage nullifies the guardianship, the stepmother will likely force Genevieve to dissolve the marriage right away."

"No." The word came out forcefully with all the protest that had been building since he'd ridden away from Genevieve. She was his, and he wouldn't let anyone change that, especially by force.

But hadn't he decided they were from two different worlds and that their lives were going in different directions? He wouldn't fit into her life. And he wouldn't ask her to give up everything to try to fit into his.

So how could they stay together? Yet how could he live without her?

He couldn't hold back a growl of frustration.

Mr. Andridge was watching him, clearly sensing the struggle. "It is easy to see that you love her for who she is and not for her wealth."

"I don't care about her money. I fell in love with her before I knew she had it."

"Exactly. She won't find many men who will be able to see past her fortune and power to be able to love her for who she truly is. If you can do that, then you're giving her an invaluable gift."

He hadn't thought about their relationship that way. But perhaps the young lawyer was right.

"And it was very clear she loves you." Mr. Andridge spoke the words with as much confidence as he had everything else.

Ryder hadn't been able to stop thinking of her declaration of love in the hotel room. And her kiss had confirmed it. If he'd had any lingering doubts, her sending a lawyer to help him fight for Boone had only proven how much she'd grown to care about him.

But what was the right thing? He'd thought he was being noble to let her go back to the life she knew. After all, she'd chosen him because she'd been vulnerable and desperate. If the situation hadn't been so difficult for her with her stepmother, she wouldn't have needed him, probably never would have been interested in a fellow like him.

Still, had he given up on them too easily?

The hollow ache in his chest radiated and reminded him that he was dying without her. He pressed his hand there, but he knew that wouldn't take away the pain. Nothing would take it away. Nothing except being with her could bring him back to life.

Mr. Andridge didn't seem to miss anything. And as he watched Ryder attempt to battle the emptiness in his chest, he smiled softly. "You don't have to lose her, Ryder."

Even if he was learning to accept the losses in his life, was this one time when he didn't have to face a loss? Could he fight for them? For her?

A tremor pulsed through him. "What can I do?"

"You're her husband. You have the power now. So go and use it."

"Go? As in go to New York City?" He couldn't do that, could he? Not with all that remained to be done on the ranch before winter. Not with having a baby. Not with the chance that she might not want to stay married to him.

Mr. Andridge pulled out his pocket watch, flipped open the case covering the face, and peered at it. "If you leave now, she'll only be one day ahead of you in her travels. And you might be able to get to her before she signs anything."

How could he leave today? But how could he delay and chance losing her forever?

An urgency began to thrum through him.

"There is no time to waste." Mr. Andridge lifted his cane and gave Ryder a push. "Go on now."

Ryder took a step back, his muscles tightening with the need to run to the stagecoach and hop aboard. But he knew he couldn't do that, had to be responsible and make arrangements for the ranch first.

Even so, his mind was already running far ahead. And he was praying he wouldn't be too late to save his marriage.

22

Genevieve paced by the fireplace, unable to stop, even though Lenora had patted the spot on the settee beside her several times. Mr. Morgan reclined in one of the wingback chairs across from Lenora and had been speaking about legal issues for the past thirty minutes since his arrival.

The parlor was as brightly lit as always, with every lantern glowing and the drapes pulled back to allow the morning sunshine to stream in and highlight the opulence of the room. All Genevieve could think about was Ryder's simple cabin and how she'd felt more love and contentment there in a short month than she had in years in her own home.

Oh, how she missed him and Boone. Without them, especially without Ryder, she was restless and could hardly think of anything or anyone else.

"That's why the marriage can be annulled," Mr.

Morgan said in his clipped tone. "Because, as your guardian, your stepmother didn't approve of the choice of your spouse."

Mr. Morgan paused and watched Genevieve, apparently expecting a comment, but she only halted her pacing and stared at the glowing coals in the stove built into the fireplace. What could she say to contradict Mr. Morgan? She'd known the lawyer and Lenora would confront her about her marriage to Ryder. She just hadn't expected it on her first full day home.

She suspected Mr. Morgan had somehow hoped to prove that her marriage to Ryder wasn't authentic. But he'd communicated with Reverend Livingston and learned that it was indeed a valid and official marriage in the state of Colorado. The only way to end it was by divorce or annulment.

"Genevieve, please sit down." Lenora's voice held a threatening note—one that had instilled fear into Genevieve in the past. But strangely, since arriving home late last night, Lenora's unspoken threats hadn't stirred the same worry as in the past.

Yes, she was afraid Lenora would find a way to harm Ryder's reputation and bring about his ruin. But during the weeklong trip back to New York City, she'd had plenty of time to think and had come to the conclusion that no matter what happened, Ryder wasn't weak and alone. He had family and friends.

If Lenora accused him of crimes and destroyed his
reputation, he'd have many people to come to his defense
and attest to what a strong and kind and honorable man
he was. Besides, his family and friends had seen him make
mistakes and had accepted and loved him anyway.

Perhaps Genevieve was also less daunted by Lenora's
threats because she'd already defied her once and had
survived on her own. Mr. Andridge's words had lingered
in her head, resounding with more power every passing
day: *If you broke free once, I suspect you can find the strength
to do it again.*

She'd thought her adventure to the West had failed,
but maybe she hadn't given herself enough credit for
escaping from Lenora's power. She had done it and had
grown as a result. She'd learned to make her own
decisions, fend for her own needs, and take care of herself.

She truly had gained strength in everything she'd
gone through. Now, in facing Lenora, she wasn't so naïve
and frightened anymore. And maybe Mr. Andridge was
right. If she'd broken free already, why couldn't she do so
again?

She had to at least try, didn't she?

Straightening her spine and drawing in a breath, she
turned. "I do thank you for coming this morning, Mr.
Morgan. But I am not ready to make any decisions yet."

"You must, Miss Hollis. It's of the utmost urgency."
Mr. Morgan tugged folded papers out of his inside coat

pocket. "I've taken the liberty of drawing up a document that would effectively annul your marriage to Ryder Oakley and make the whole mess disappear from your records."

She had explicitly trusted Mr. Morgan since her papa's death, had believed he was looking out for her. In fact, she'd trusted him more than Lenora, had always taken everything he'd said to be truthful and sincere.

But now? After how he'd negated her request for the best lawyer in Denver and had sought out the opposite to undermine her efforts? She had to be cautious with him as well as with Lenora.

Thankfully, Mr. Andridge had been honest enough to bring Mr. Morgan's faults to her attention. When she'd arrived home last night, she'd hoped to have a telegram from Mr. Andridge waiting for her—one announcing the outcome of the custody proceedings. But there hadn't been any correspondence.

She was growing impatient for the news and had decided that after the meeting with Lenora and Mr. Morgan, she would instruct Emmett to take her to the telegram office, and she wouldn't leave until she'd heard back from Mr. Andridge.

In fact, Emmett was waiting for her in the hallway, just outside the parlor door. During the whole train ride back from Colorado, he'd hardly left her side. Although he was gruff with others, he'd treated her with the utmost care and consideration at all times and had been much more personable with her than the other bodyguard.

After spending nearly every minute with him for the past week, she'd grown to appreciate him and even held a fondness for him. Last night when he'd delivered her home, she'd asked him if he'd like to stay on as a permanent member of the staff. Lenora had opposed it, but Genevieve had surprised herself by insisting. And she'd been even more surprised when Emmett had defied Lenora and accepted the position.

Genevieve wasn't sure exactly how long Emmett would be able to keep the position before Lenora forced him out, but for now, she felt as though she had at least one ally.

Regardless of his presence, it was still up to her to clarify to both Lenora and Mr. Morgan that her marriage to Ryder may have started as one of convenience, the answering of a newspaper advertisement, but it had turned into so much more.

The truth was that the distance from Ryder hadn't dimmed her feelings for him. Instead, it had only served to bring into better focus all the qualities she loved about him. At the top of the list was how he'd shouldered being a single father to Boone and had done so with patience and gentleness and sweetness.

His love for his child was enough to win her heart, but he'd won it in other ways too. He was resilient, strong, and determined which was the reason he'd survived all that he had in his life. And he treated the people he loved with such devotion and loyalty.

As if that weren't enough, he'd also taken the news of her deception calmly, much more so than any other man would have—especially a man who'd already been abandoned once by a wife. He'd listened to her explanations, humbled himself, and accepted his role in all that had transpired.

How could she walk away from a man like that and relinquish him forever? How could she even relinquish him for a short while?

She closed her eyes to fight the hopelessness that came with just thinking about giving him up. She couldn't do it. She knew deep in her soul she'd never find another man like Ryder Oakley, who loved her for who she was as a woman, faults and all. He wasn't enamored of her wealth or prestige and wasn't caught up trying to please her or tell her what she wanted to hear or impress her to win her affection. No, he was himself, and that was enough.

"If you'll sign here at the bottom of the second page . . ." Mr. Morgan said.

She opened her eyes to find him standing in front of her, the sheets unfolded, and a pen in one hand. Something in the strength of his stance and the firmness of his mouth told her he wouldn't be swayed.

Lenora was on her feet now too, her body rigid. "As I told you, Genevieve, if you comply, then I won't need to punish Ryder Oakley and his family for colluding together to swindle you out of your fortune."

At this newest threat—not just against Ryder, but now toward his whole family—a chill crept up Genevieve's spine. She wanted to lift her chin and shout at Lenora that the Oakleys were innocent, but it would do no good. None of her pleas had mattered when she'd tried to save Prescott and his father from ruin.

Lenora took the sheet from Mr. Morgan and thrust it in front of Genevieve. "As your guardian, I command you to sign the annulment."

Mr. Morgan held out the pen.

Genevieve kept both of her arms stiffly at her sides, fear battling with her love and need for Ryder. As she stared down at the paper, overwhelming protest swelled inside. She couldn't—wouldn't—end her marriage to Ryder, regardless of the consequences. Whatever happened, she would find new strength to overcome the obstacles.

"Mr. Morgan, Lenora." She took a step back. "I love my husband and am staying married to him."

The two exchanged a look—one that told Genevieve they'd conferred over the options and were prepared to continue to fight her and likely would issue more threats in an attempt to break her resolve.

She twisted the simple wedding band on her finger, which had become more precious to her than any other piece of jewelry she owned. She'd forgotten to give it back to Ryder when they'd parted ways. Or maybe, deep inside, she'd known all along that she wouldn't be able to end her marriage.

Lenora wrapped her fingers around Genevieve's arm and pinched hard. "You have no choice, Genevieve. If you don't sign the annulment, Mr. Morgan has lined up a judge who is willing to declare you mentally unstable, and I'll need to commit you to an asylum until you come to your senses."

Genevieve quavered. Their plan was dreadful. But she'd much rather have them attack her than Ryder. "I will not sign."

Lenora's eyes glittered with her anger. "I have sacrificed much to raise you, and I'll not have you take away what I deserve."

She held Lenora's gaze, hoping to prove that she wouldn't cower. "What do you deserve?"

"Your father left me nothing in his will."

"That's not true. He allocated enough for your needs."

"I deserve more, much more. And I intend to continue to take as much as I can until next year."

Had Lenora discovered a way to access the Hollis fortune already? How?

Mr. Morgan shook his head, as though warning Lenora not to say anything more.

Genevieve's chest tightened. Of course that was how. With Mr. Morgan's help.

Lenora wasn't watching Mr. Morgan, was standing too close to Genevieve to see the warning. "And I won't let your hasty marriage stop me from being your guardian—not when we still have a dozen sales pending."

"Sales pending?"

"Lenora." Mr. Morgan spoke sharply.

This time, Lenora pressed her lips together.

But it was too late. Even though Genevieve didn't understand everything, she could guess what Lenora was doing. She was selling off her papa's assets and businesses and was probably giving Mr. Morgan a share of the profits.

Genevieve didn't care about any of it—didn't care if they sold every home, every business, every yacht, and every jewel. "You know I don't care about my papa's fortune, and I would have given you more if you'd asked me."

"After all I've done for you, I do deserve more." Lenora's voice held a note of bitterness. "But your father only gave me a pittance."

"So you're finding ways to steal from me?" The words slipped out before Genevieve could filter them.

Lenora lifted a hand and swiftly slapped Genevieve's cheek.

The sound echoed in the silence, and the sting startled Genevieve. Lenora had only ever slapped her one other time—that day she'd tried to defend Prescott. The slap had frightened Genevieve then, but it only fueled determination inside her now.

"Don't touch Mrs. Oakley again," came Emmett's hard voice from near the doorway, followed by the heavy thud of his footsteps crossing the room. His expression was as grave as always, his eyes trained upon Lenora with a deadliness that was frightening.

Genevieve wrenched her arm free from Lenora. "I want you and Mr. Morgan to leave my house now."

Lenora reached for Genevieve again. "As your guardian, I'm legally in charge of this house and of you."

In the next instant, Emmett was stepping in front of Genevieve and using his large frame to blockade Lenora. "I think you'd better listen to Mrs. Oakley."

"I don't take orders from anyone." Lenora stiffened and gave Emmett her haughtiest glare. "Not from my stepdaughter, and certainly not from hired help."

Emmett crossed his arms over his chest, clearly not intimidated by Lenora. "When you hired me, you told me I needed to protect Mrs. Oakley from herself. But it's become clear she needs protection from you."

Mr. Morgan stood behind Lenora, now holding the

annulment paper and the pen.

Lenora glared at Emmett. "Just you wait. I will destroy you."

He didn't budge.

"As soon as this meeting is adjourned, I shall be summoning the police department to arrest you for stealing from us."

"I'll be making a visit of my own to the police department to let them know about your underhanded dealings with Mrs. Oakley, like stealing her telegrams." Emmett slipped an envelope into Genevieve's hand. "This was delivered earlier this morning, but Mrs. Hollis instructed me not to give it to you and to destroy it."

Lenora tried to grab the envelope. "That's private information—"

"It was addressed to Mrs. Oakley." Emmett side-stepped, blocking Lenora again.

A telegram? The one she'd been waiting for from Mr. Andridge regarding Ryder and Boone?

In spite of the tenseness of the moment at hand, she needed to find out what had happened. The envelope had already been opened, and no doubt Lenora had intercepted the telegram and read it. Genevieve could only pray the message contained good news, otherwise, why would Lenora have wanted to prevent her from seeing it?

As Genevieve slipped the telegram out, her fingers

shook. The message was from Mr. Andridge and was short and to the point: *Sadie gave up rights. Ryder has permanent custody.*

A rush of joy filled her, and tears clouded her eyes so that she could hardly read the rest of the telegram: *Do not dissolve the marriage. It voids the guardianship.*

She blinked and read the last line again, trying to comprehend Mr. Andridge's words. Was he telling her that because she was now married, her stepmother no longer had any authority over her? That the guardianship was no longer binding or legal?

Lenora and Mr. Morgan continued arguing with Emmett, their voices swirling around her, but she didn't listen to anything they were saying. The only thing going through her head was that Lenora had no power over her. She was free. Finally free.

No wonder they were trying so fervently to get her to sign the annulment papers. Because she was married, Lenora was done, no longer had a place in Genevieve's life or her home.

"I want you to leave." The words slipped out, and as soon as they did, everyone grew silent.

Emmett shifted to look at her. His expression remained severe, but his brows rose.

She could sense that he was asking her what he could do to help her. Relief swelled within her that she didn't have to battle Lenora and Mr. Morgan alone, that

Emmett had no fear of Lenora and was coming to her defense.

"Mr. Morgan, I am firing you as my lawyer." She spoke louder this time, letting new strength rise within her. "I no longer need your services and will have my new lawyer contact you this morning." She hoped Mr. Andridge would take on the responsibility. But even if he didn't, she couldn't trust Mr. Morgan ever again.

"There's no need to be hasty about such a decision." Mr. Morgan had already folded the papers and was slipping them back into his pocket. "Think about what your father, your dear papa, would want you to do."

"He would want me to be strong enough to fight for myself. And that is what I am doing."

Mr. Morgan had the decency not to respond.

What had changed him from a friend to a foe? Maybe he never had truly been as trustworthy as either her papa or she had believed. Or maybe greed had darkened his heart. Whatever had happened, she never wanted to see him again.

Genevieve turned her attention upon her stepmother. "Lenora, you have one hour to pack your bags and leave my house. If you're not gone, Emmett will escort you out."

Emmett gave Genevieve a curt nod, his eyes holding approval for her decisions. And she knew then that she'd found the strength she needed to take back her life. Now she just needed to find the strength to reclaim Ryder and make a way for their marriage to work.

She wasn't sure how to bridge the distance or their differences, but she did know she had to try. Even if that meant traveling back to Colorado and living there until she could convince him that she wanted to make their marriage permanent.

23

Ryder lifted a fist to the thick oak door of the brownstone mansion. Then he paused, his knuckles skimming the wood.

What was he doing here? What right did he think he had, walking up the steps to Genevieve's home in New York City and knocking on her door?

He didn't belong here. Not in the city and especially not in this neighborhood of massive reddish-brown sandstone homes four or five stories high, with elaborate details, tall arched doorways, elongated windows, elegant stoops, wrought-iron fencing, and ground-floor servant's entrances.

Everything was perfect and clean and well-maintained and spoke of a lifestyle that was far removed from everything he'd ever known. The street was swept clean of the usual residue, had fancy lampposts evenly spaced, and even had a few saplings with changing leaves.

Had he made a mistake in coming? Should he get a room in a hotel for the night first? After all, it was late in the day, with the darkness of evening beginning to settle. He was grimy from the traveling and needed to bathe and change into clean garments first.

His life had been a whirlwind since that morning meeting with Mr. Andridge, Mr. Irving, and Sadie. He'd left Breckenridge and gone directly to High C Ranch to plead with Maverick to help him with his ranch while he was away—to send a couple of his ranch hands to look after the place and finish the harvest. He'd been instructing Maverick to sell a couple of heads of cattle to pay for the expenses during his absence when Tanner had arrived and joined in making the plans.

The plans had included Tanner riding east too, so that he could meet with his investigator face-to-face and visit the orphanages they'd once lived at in order to dig for more information.

Ryder could feel Tanner's gaze boring into him as he turned away from the door.

"Where are you going?" came Tanner's voice from the carriage. "You came all this way; now talk to her."

Ryder halted, one foot poised above the top step, and scowled at his brother sitting in the dark shadows of the carriage with Boone on his lap. He was grateful Tanner had insisted on coming along, but at times like this, his brother was too forward and bossy and needed to leave him alone to figure things out.

"At least let her know you're here," Tanner called.

Ryder hesitated, then pivoted and forced himself to knock, this time making contact with the door. The entire train ride, he'd done little else but think about what he would say. He'd come all this way to tell her he couldn't live without her—that he didn't just want a mother for his son; he wanted a wife.

But now, after seeing her home and getting a true picture of the reality of their differences, every word he'd planned seemed inadequate.

He was inadequate for her. Why had he ever thought he could be enough?

Before he could convince himself to walk away, the door swung open to reveal an elderly butler.

Ryder squared his shoulders.

With a stoic expression, the butler swept his gaze over Ryder. "May I help you?"

Ryder peered past the man to a long, brightly lit entryway. His body keened for the sight of Genevieve. In fact, he was suddenly desperate to see her, to hold her, to have her back. The past week and a half without her had been the longest week and a half of his life.

He wanted to shove past the butler and call out for her, but he forced himself to take a breath and answer politely. "I'd like to see Genevieve. My wife."

The butler's eyes widened.

"Please," Ryder added. Tanner had coached him all the way from the train depot on the proper manners to use and how to present himself as a gentleman. He wasn't sure how Tanner knew, but Ryder was determined to be the kind of man Genevieve could be proud of.

Of course, anyone who looked at him closely enough would realize he wasn't really a gentleman, even though he was wearing his church clothing and looked less like a rancher and more like a business owner.

After several long heartbeats, the butler backed up and waved Ryder inside.

As Ryder stepped through the door and into the narrow entry hall, he had a sense that he'd been there before—or a place like it. The stairway with the dark banister, the speckled marble tile, the high ceiling with the carved cornices—it all seemed so familiar.

His mind flashed to an image of him with Tanner, racing down a stairway and jumping into the arms of a large man. A woman holding a violin was rushing out of the double doors of a side room. *"Hawthorne, darling."*

"Father." The word whispered through Ryder. He could almost hear himself as a boy, saying the word as the man's arms surrounded him and hugged him tight.

Ryder tried to picture the man's face, but as with the nightmare, he couldn't see any features. Everything was all empty, like blank frames awaiting photographs that needed to be developed.

Was Hawthorne his father's name? And had his family once lived in a home like this? Was that why it felt strangely familiar?

He looked around again, trying to hold on to the memories, trying to make them come even more to life so that he could share them with Tanner. Even as the visions of the past faded, the name Hawthorne lingered. Surely a unique name such as Hawthorne would give Tanner's investigator more to go on than just Sarah, Edward, and Donny.

"Where is my wife?" He tried to keep the gruffness from his voice, but it ended up there anyway. His *wife*. The one word held more meaning than he'd ever thought possible. But that was what she was. His wife. And he wanted her so much that he knew he'd give up everything to be with her, including the ranch.

Yes, he loved having his own place, but that's all it was. A place on the map. Maybe all his losses in life had honed his perspective and shown him that people were more important than anything he could own. And anything she owned.

All he really wanted was her. He could make a life anywhere as long as he was with her.

"Miss Hollis—" The butler halted abruptly. "I mean, Mrs. Oakley has just left and won't be back for several weeks, perhaps longer."

Ryder's pulse slammed to a halt. "Left? Where?" The

house did seem too quiet for the evening hour, the usual clatter from the kitchen and the scents of a cooking meal absent.

"She is going—" At the bang of a back door and footsteps racing up a rear stairway, the butler spun and started down the hallway.

"I have forgotten my heaviest coat," came Genevieve's call. "And I shall need it there. It was already cold when I left and will only get colder."

Without moving, Ryder waited breathlessly for his first sight of her. As she entered the hallway, he could only take her in hungrily. She was more beautiful than he remembered, with her delicate features, pale skin, and blue-gray eyes. She had on a blue gown with a back bustle that swished with each step she took. Her dark hair was coiled in loose ringlets, and an elegant hat was perched atop her head. Clearly she was getting ready to go out for the evening.

She rushed forward. "Could you help me find it, Ambrose?"

When the butler didn't respond but instead cocked his head toward the front door, Genevieve's gaze swung to Ryder.

She halted and gasped, lifting a gloved hand to her mouth as if to capture her surprise. In the next instant, her eyes glistened and tears began to slip down her cheeks.

His chest swelled, and heat stung the backs of his eyes

too. He started toward her. Nothing else mattered but gathering her in his arms and never letting her leave him again.

24

Ryder was here. In her home.

Genevieve was too shocked to move. He'd come all the way across the country. For her.

His footsteps lengthened as he crossed toward her, and she could see it in his eyes with each step. He wanted her and nothing else mattered.

He was all that mattered to her too.

She dropped her hand, released a small cry, then flew toward him.

His arms wrapped around her at the same time as she flung hers around his neck. He drew her body against his in a crushing embrace—one that held all his love and desire. He left her no doubt about it.

Sobs swelled in her chest, tightening her throat.

This was where she needed to be . . . in his arms. And she never wanted to be any place else. He was her home now.

His hands were tight against her back and held her as though he never planned to release her either. And that was fine with her. He could hold her all the time, and she'd never grow weary of it.

"I've missed you so much." She sniffled and pulled back so that she could see his handsome face. His hair was neatly combed and his beard trimmed short, giving him an almost aristocratic look. His eyes were dark and full of heat, so that the merest look melted her insides and made her nothing more than a puddle in his arms.

He didn't say the words in return, but he bent in and let his lips touch hers. The sweetness of tasting him again after so long was more than she'd anticipated, and she found herself greedily responding to him.

As if her welcome was the invitation to lose himself in her every bit as she was in him, he delved in deeper, his need for her containing an urgency that matched hers. They'd almost lost each other, had nearly been ripped apart. And now his kiss was surely his way of telling her that he didn't want that to happen ever again. . . . At least, she hoped it was.

As if he'd heard her thoughts, he broke the kiss and pulled back enough that he was peering into her eyes, his gaze as intense as always. "I need you to stay married to me in order to keep your stepmother from getting her guardianship back."

She pinched her eyes closed to block out how

A WIFE FOR THE RANCHER

disastrously this morning could have gone—had almost gone. Thankfully, she'd realized Lenora and Mr. Morgan were scheming before it was too late, and thankfully Emmett had been there to defend her and give her Mr. Andridge's telegram.

He'd continued to defend her all throughout the afternoon too. He'd made sure Lenora left within an hour. And he'd sent for the chief of police so that Genevieve could relay all that had happened and file charges against Lenora and Mr. Morgan. The chief of police had given her the references of several local lawyers, and although she'd contacted them, she'd also sent a telegram to Mr. Andridge, inviting him to become her primary lawyer and relocate to New York City.

His answer had come nearly right away: *Yes. Honored to be your advocate and friend.*

To say she'd been relieved was an understatement, especially when one of Mr. Morgan's aides had brought over a file holding all the sales Mr. Morgan and Lenora had already made with her papa's investments and businesses. Another file had contained the pending sales worth thousands upon thousands of dollars.

She knew there would be much to sort through in the coming days to repair all the damage. But that hadn't stopped her from packing her bags and making arrangements to leave for Colorado on the last train of the day.

Emmett had insisted on traveling with her. He'd followed her back inside, and she knew he was nearby but being discreet and allowing her a semblance of privacy. Ambrose had also stepped into one of the side rooms the moment she'd reunited with Ryder.

"You haven't already dissolved the marriage, have you?" Ryder's voice was low and distressed.

"No." She offered what she hoped was a reassuring smile. "Lenora and Mr. Morgan tried, but they couldn't make me."

He leaned his forehead against hers. "So you'll agree to staying married for your sake?"

She loved the feel of his head against hers, the mingling of their breaths, and the hard pattering of their heartbeats. But she wasn't agreeing to what he was offering. "No."

He tried to lift his head, likely to protest.

But she wove her fingers through his hair to keep him where he was. "The only way I'll agree to stay married is for *our* sake, Ryder. Because we both want it."

His shoulders relaxed, and his forehead rested against hers again.

"I want to stay married to you," she continued, "because I'm so in love with you that I can't imagine going another day without being your wife."

His hand at the small of her back pressed her in tighter.

"Those are my terms," she whispered, her lips so close to his. "Are you agreeable?"

"Yes." His whisper was soft, reverent. And when he touched his lips to hers, they were soft and reverent too, letting her know in a way that words couldn't convey that he couldn't imagine going another day without her by his side either.

25

Ryder had never pictured himself being content sitting at a desk and poring over business ledgers and records, but with every passing day of learning more about Mr. Hollis's business investments and ventures, he found that his interest was only growing.

"And I've contacted three more of the financial advisors earlier today," Mr. Andridge was saying from the chair across the desk from Ryder. "They'll be giving me a detailed report on all the transactions."

The young lawyer had arrived in New York City a week ago and plunged right into the disaster that Mr. Morgan had made with his underhanded sales. Mr. Andridge had not only begun finding ways to recover what had been lost but had also taken over prosecuting Mr. Morgan and Lenora for their swindling. But the process was complicated and would likely take months.

At a soft knocking against the door frame, Ryder's

heartbeat began to race. He didn't even have to look to know who was there. But he liked looking at his wife. In fact, he liked looking at her a lot.

He crossed his arms behind his head and sat back in the leather chair that had once belonged to Mr. Hollis. He'd initially been drawn to the office because of the floor-to-ceiling bookshelves along one wall, filled with an incredible collection of history books that Genevieve had given to him as a wedding present.

There were still times he couldn't believe they were married and she was his wife. He let his gaze rove over her, starting with her dark hair, pretty, smiling lips, flushed cheeks, and then working his way down, lingering on her beautiful body.

She offered a polite smile to Mr. Andridge, but then she turned her gaze back to Ryder. "Boone is napping for a while this afternoon."

Her gaze raked over his body in the same way his had just raked hers, leaving a trail burning through him—a hot trail he wouldn't be able to extinguish, a hot trail he only wanted to fuel all the more.

He dropped his arms from behind his head and tapped the desk in front of him. "Good. Do you have a minute to give me your opinion on something?"

"Of course." Her smile only widened.

Although he didn't grin, pleasure rippled through him. He'd loved being with her for the past two weeks since his arrival. It had been pure bliss both day and night. And he especially loved stolen moments like this.

"I guess this is my cue to leave." Mr. Andridge stood with his silver cane, his voice wry with humor. He'd witnessed their affection for each other enough since arriving and had shown himself to be tactful, which Ryder appreciated.

It didn't take long for Mr. Andridge to gather his files and head out of the office. As the door clicked closed behind him, Genevieve was already at Ryder's side. "So, you would like my expert opinion, would you?"

He fitted his hands on her waist and dragged her down so that she was sitting on his lap. Her arms wound around his neck, and she quickly bent in, her gaze riveted to his mouth, one thing clearly on her mind.

Kissing her was always on his mind. He could admit it. And as she closed the last of the distance, he wasted no time in giving them both what they wanted, fusing their lips with a fervor that was filled with all his adoration for both her body and spirit. He'd never tire of showing her how much he cherished her, had decided it was something that would take forever and that he'd relish every moment.

At the bang of the door opening, Genevieve startled and would have stood up except that he held her in place. Only one person ever interrupted them so boldly. Tanner.

"Don't you ever do anything else besides kiss?"

Tanner's voice dripped with sarcasm as he leaned against the doorframe.

"Don't you ever knock?" Ryder groused back.

"Not when it's so fun to interrupt you."

Ryder fitted Genevieve into the crook of his arm and loved that she didn't fight him, instead curling into him with her head resting against his shoulder. "One of these days, I'll pay you back. Just wait."

He hoped Tanner would have the good fortune of finding a woman as wonderful as Genevieve. In the meantime, Tanner had been busy most of the time, visiting orphanages, searching records, and working with his investigators to track down leads. Now that they believed their father's name was Hawthorne, they'd hoped that would help, but so far, they'd gotten nowhere in their search.

Tanner didn't come inside. His expression held an intensity that made Ryder sit up straighter, forcing Genevieve to do the same. "What is it?"

"It's time for me to head back." After arriving in New York City, Tanner had shaven, gotten a hair trim, and shed his coonskin cap and buckskin coat for a regular hat and suit, probably so that he'd have more luck and face less discrimination during his investigations. But today, he wore his usual mountain-man attire.

"You sure?" Even as Ryder asked the question, he realized that he was the uncertain one, not Tanner. He wasn't ready to let go of his brother. Tanner was all he had left of his past, and he didn't want to lose him, even if only to distance.

"I'm sure." Tanner met his gaze, a sadness and a maturity in his eyes that hadn't been there before. Probably because he was starting to finally realize just how impossible tracking down their family was and was learning to accept the inevitable—that they didn't have anyone else left, only each other.

Tanner straightened his cap and then slung his bag over his shoulder. "I want to get back into the high country before snow closes up the passes."

"You've never let a little snow stop you before."

"I know. But it's time for me to go."

Ryder's gut tightened.

Genevieve laid one of her hands on his, obviously sensing his unrest.

He wanted to say that he'd be back at his own ranch soon and would see Tanner then, but he hadn't made up his mind yet when to leave New York City. A part of him knew he would need to go soon too now that it was early October.

But another part of him wanted to stay and work with Mr. Andridge and continue to learn more about the Hollis enterprises. Genevieve had also introduced him to a publisher who was interested in helping him polish and publish his collection of tales that told the history of Colorado.

Genevieve had assured him that she would be happy to go with him wherever he chose, that she didn't have a preference either way. Even so, he'd noticed the way she glowed whenever she came back from volunteering at the orphanage. And she'd resumed many of the charities that Lenora had cancelled and now spent much of her free time overseeing their operation.

"You need to stay." Tanner spoke the words with such conviction that this time Ryder startled.

"I haven't decided—"

"You belong here." Tanner waved at the office and the desk and then at Genevieve. "It's almost as if you were made for this."

"But my ranch—"

"It was never your passion. You did it because you had to provide for your family."

Was Tanner right?

"And you did it so that you could stay close to me." Tanner's eyes gleamed with unshed tears that he rapidly blinked away. "But I don't need you to watch out for me any longer, Ryder. I'll be okay. I want you to be free to lead your own life and find your own happiness now."

Ryder's throat tightened with emotion. Was that what he'd been doing? Watching out for Tanner all these years and putting his own life on hold to do so?

Tanner held his gaze a final long moment, then nodded.

"Goodbye, Tanner." Genevieve smiled at him tenderly. "You know you're always welcome here."

"Thank you." He seemed to be taking in her beauty. "I'm glad Ryder has you now. You're the family he's always needed."

Without another word, Tanner spun and walked away.

Ryder watched the open door, not quite ready to let him go but knowing he had to.

Genevieve didn't say anything—just leaned her head back against his shoulder while still holding his hand.

Tanner was right. It was time for them to go their own ways and make something of themselves. They'd both been spared to live. And it was time to start doing that to the fullest.

He bent and pressed a kiss against Genevieve's forehead. "I love you."

She lifted his hand and kissed the back of it. "I love you too."

He was living his life to the fullest with her. He couldn't ask for anything better.

Author's Note

Dear Reader,

I absolutely adore mail-order bride stories. Add a rich heiress on the run, and the story is even more fun, wouldn't you agree? I hope you enjoyed reading Ryder and Genevieve's story as much as I enjoyed writing it.

I also really loved delving more into Ryder's and Tanner's background. Will the two adopted brothers find their long-lost family and get closure on their past? Or will they finally learn to accept the tragedies of their childhood so that they can move on and embrace the future? I hope you'll read Tanner's story in the next book to find out.

As always, I love hearing from YOU! If you haven't yet joined my Facebook Reader Room, what are you waiting for!? It's a great place to keep up to date on all my book releases and book news, as well as a fun place to connect with other readers and me.

Until next time . . .

Make sure you didn't miss out on any other books in the High Country Ranch series. Here's a complete list of all the books. They can be read as standalones, but they're even better read in order.

Waiting for the Rancher

Hazel Noble loves her job managing the mares at High Country Ranch. As the foaling season begins, she gets to spend even more time with the horses . . . and with her secret crush, Maverick Oakley, the owner of High Country Ranch and her brother Sterling's best friend. When Maverick unwittingly ruins Sterling's wedding, he goes from best friend to worst enemy. With the rift between their families, Maverick is faced with the possibility of losing Hazel, and he can no longer deny how much he's always cared about her.

Willing to Wed the Rancher

Assistant schoolteacher Clarabelle Oakley has a hard time saying no. When Eric Meyer, widowed father of two of her young students, proposes to her, she botches her effort to tell him no and that she wants to marry for love, not convenience. Only days later, the unthinkable happens, and Clarabelle learns she's been given charge of Eric's children and his farm. Professor Franz Meyer arrives in Summit County, Colorado, to make peace with his estranged brother but discovers Eric is gone, leaving too many unanswered questions.

A Wife for the Rancher

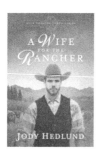

Millionaire heiress, Genevieve Hollis, has everything she wants except one thing, freedom, because her guardian stepmother insists on overseeing every move she makes. When Genevieve sees a newspaper advertisement from a rancher seeking a mother for his baby, she jumps at the chance to escape. Ryder Oakley has suffered the repeated misfortune of losing the people he loves most, so now that he's a single father with a newborn baby, he's determined not to lose his son.

Wrangling the Wandering Rancher

Maisy Merritt has vowed she'll never marry a mountain man. Even though she loves the Colorado Rockies and the wild creatures she helps, she hates the way her pa's mountain-man ways take him away from his family. Maisy's ready to start a normal life, and that includes marrying a normal man. As a trapper and trail guide, Tanner Oakley lives a wandering life. He's decided that he's not husband material for any woman since he's so restless and unsettled.

Wishing for the Rancher's Love

As the only one of her siblings who hasn't married, Clementine Oakley feels left behind. But she does her best to focus on her candy-making business in Worth's General Store. Giving and outgoing, she makes friends with everyone—except one person, the store owner's son . . . Grady Worth. Grady isn't sure why he can't get along with Clementine, but every time they're together, all they do is bicker. When his dad proposes a contest to encourage Grady to find love, Clementine is the last person he considers as an option.

Jody Hedlund is the bestselling author of more than fifty novels and is the winner of numerous awards. Jody lives in Michigan with her husband, busy family, and five spoiled cats. She writes sweet historical romances with plenty of sizzle.

A complete list of my novels can be found at jodyhedlund.com.

Would you like to know when my next book is available? You can sign up for my newsletter, become my friend on Goodreads, like me on Facebook, or follow me on Instagram.

Newsletter: jodyhedlund.com

Facebook: AuthorJodyHedlund

Instagram: @JodyHedlund

Made in the USA
Las Vegas, NV
07 October 2024

96381373R00173